Whispering Shadows

Also by Rose Helen Mitchell and published by Ginninderra Press
Siege of Contraries
Pilgrim Souls
Across Time & Place (Pocket Poets)
James Joyce, Ulysses & Ireland (Pocket Polemics)
Pasha (Pocket People)

Rose Helen Mitchell

Whispering Shadows

Acknowledgements

Thanks to my daughter Anne Marie James and to my sister
Evelyn O'Daly for their astute judgement and insight.

Thanks also to Pat and John Whelan for their constant support and generous
offer of their family's beachside retreat, where miracles can happen.

Special thanks to Stephen and Brenda Matthews
at Ginninderra Press for their encouragement and patience
during the production of this book. The many cups of tea and
enlightening conversations made the journey pleasant and productive.

Whispering Shadows
ISBN 978 1 74027 849 2

First published 2014
Reprinted 2017

GINNINDERRA PRESS
PO Box 3461 Port Adelaide 5015
www.ginninderrapress.com.au

Contents

To the people of all ages and many nationalities
who have enriched my life

Whispering shadows

While we waited for my father to return from the war a hero, we lived in a big old place with high ceilings, long passages and lots of cubbyholes. It was a great haunt, where my brother and sisters and I played hide and seek on rainy days. At one time, it had been the local priest's house and the smell of candle wax and lavender polish seemed to leak from the walls and wooden floors. The living room was the nicest room in the house. It had big bumphly cushions on a fat couch and fatter chairs. A fireplace, nearly the length of one wall, had a wooden mantel shelf above it and on the centre of this shelf, my father's face looked down to me from a shiny brass frame.

His officer's uniform was trimmed with gold braid and insignia that didn't mean much to me then. I used to think that his eyes followed me and sometimes I'd tell him about what games we'd been playing or what we'd had for dinner. Our house was the last house on a street that bordered open fields where women like my mother planted and harvested potatoes, tomatoes, rhubarb, turnips – whatever was in season – for destinations that we read about but never saw.

My mother was tall and slim. She had a mop of dark, unruly hair and wonderful eyes that shone when she was happy. She liked working in Mr Kerr's tomato houses. The extra money helped and we got free tomatoes that she stuffed down the front of her dungarees when she thought Kerr wasn't looking. I loved to hear her stories about riding to the farm in the lorry that had seen better days. She would tell us about the cheery banter amongst the women, how they'd rather be wearing slinky satin dresses and silk stockings instead of men's working garb, and how farmer Kerr had said, 'There's not a muscle among you lot.' The dungarees that their husbands had exchanged for khaki were handy containers for contraband vegetables and the women laughed off Kerr's resentment and chauvinism while sneaking his produce into their overalls.

When I couldn't get to sleep, Mum would tell me stories about when she and Dad first met and the fun they'd had decorating and furnishing their first small house. Then she'd say, 'Your dad's not fighting with guns at the front, he's repairing damage to ships, and that's a safe job in these times.' At school assembly, when we were asked to pray for somebody's father or uncle who had died or posted as missing presumed dead, I remembered this. I didn't want my father to be a war hero – I just wanted him to come home to us and make my mother laugh again.

Sometimes when we came home from school, my mother would meet us at the door, excited. 'We've got more treats from Australia. We'll open it when everyone's here.'

I'd race down the street to tell my tardy siblings, 'Stop dilly-dallying. We've got a parcel from Dad.'

These parcels had luxuries that we could never get because of the rationing. There'd be packets of sultanas, raisins, figs, tins of Bartlett pears and canned ham. We boasted to neighbour children about the goodies we had and my mother baked yummy fruit cakes. One parcel had a card and some photos. The card was an invitation from the 'Directors of David Jones' to a 'Dinner Dance' in honour of the visiting 'British Fleet' in the 'Great Restaurant' of their main store in Sydney on 22 February 1945.

'Your father loves to dance. I'll bet he enjoyed that night. We used to dance so well together,' my mother said. 'We met at a dinner dance, you know.' As she spoke, anxious battle lines vanished from her face and her voice seemed to come from deep in her throat. 'I danced most of the night with your father. He was the best-looking man in the hall and my escort for the party never talked to me again.'

I had only seen my father for a short time and barely knew him, but I remembered the smell and touch of his uniform and the smoothness of his white shirt at his last farewell.

In the late summer of 1945, the crops in the fields that surrounded the village were as high as my head and ready for harvesting. Flattened patches could be seen where wayward children had sat and rubbed the heads of grain in their hands before blowing away the chaff and devouring the sweet, fresh kernels. The season's wild roses that edged the fields lay composting while their legacy of rose hips waited on hedgerows to be picked and sold for pocket money. On the roadsides, bushes of wild gooseberries and purplish-black brambles made feasts for Sunday walkers and jam for breakfast toast and Mum's flaky pastry turnovers.

In the gloaming of summer nights, we played on the oval in front of our house until late. Sometimes we put on a variety show in the air raid shelter that had been put up at the beginning of the war. It was never used as a shelter but young couples needing a private corner for kissing and cuddling often sidled in as if nobody saw them. At these concerts we'd charge tuppence or thruppence entry fee. We told people this was to help the war effort but, as we usually only had about five paying people in the audience, we spent the money in Jim McKinstry's fish and chip shop.

One day, we got a letter from Dad with a photo that showed him with two of his shipmates. They were accompanied by three young women in clingy, shiny dresses and corsages pinned at their shoulders. The fairest of the women was standing with one shoulder touching my father and her head leaned towards him. Someone had written on the back, 'Dinner Dance, Sydney Feb 1945'.

Not long after that, on a night when I had trouble sleeping, I crept along to the living room. A soft light glowing from a candle burning in front of my father's photo seeped around my mother's face. She sat facing his image as if she was willing him to appear in the flesh out of the flame. She took me in her arms and held me so close that I nearly broke in half.

By late 1945 there was still no news of my father's homecoming. Celebrations for VE day and VJ day had come and gone and welcome home parties had started in our village. Houses decorated with bunting and banners waved a greeting to returning servicemen. Blackout blinds no longer shut out the world and nosey folk were again able to look into other people's lives through naked windows. Streetlights were lit again and they were an object of wonder to me. I would stand under them, studying how they cast shadows on the pathway. I'd dance around the circle of light moving my arms and legs to make grotesque shapes that were meant to be ducks or rabbits. On some evenings, if the temperature was right, a mist would gather around the light in a mysterious halo. I used to try and conjure images of my father through the mist. I'd pretend that he had talked to me and I'd tell him about the concerts and how Mum made the best fruit cakes and jam.

Joe Cassidy returned from the war on the day of my sixth birthday; and the two events are still entangled in my mind. On the evening of that day, the villagers congregated near the Black Bull tavern at the southern end of the village. The community's only taxi had gone to collect him from the train station and people congregated at the gate of his house with accordions, fiddles and whistles. I remember still the music of that night and how the feet flashed and stomped and glided across and around the tarmac dance floor. My mother stood with a group of neighbours, listening and speculating about the end of things like food rationing, gas masks, identity cards. We played hide-and-seek amongst the adults and old men compared the taste and smell of Virginian cigarettes with the vile Turkish brand they'd been limited to during the war.

Parcels stopped coming from Australia. The HMS *Resource* had been requisitioned as a troop ship and still no word from my father. We made up stories to our friends that he'd joined the Americans and we'd soon be leaving for Kentucky or Seattle. Or that my father was lost in the jungle at Guadalcanal, or his ship had got sunk. We lied.

We came home from school one day to find Mrs Hunter and Mrs Cummings consoling my mother. She was sobbing and twisting her hankie together with a letter in her hands. Her face was so white it looked like the blood from her cheeks had been pumped into her red and swollen eyes.

Later that day, we were told, 'Your father's not coming home. He's made a new life with another family in Australia. We're on our own now.'

The noise of my world disintegrating stopped in my ears for a long, long time and there were shadows wherever I looked.

Much later, on a day when rain battered against our windows and the house seemed full of ghosts, the photo of the Sydney dinner dance fell at my feet in shreds.

My big brother Ben held me close and said, 'Hush now, hush…we need to think of Mum now.'

There were heroes everywhere in those days but my father wasn't amongst them and the shadows that whispered around me then shaped all of my future.

Legacy

The morning of my tenth birthday began with Mum and me leafing through the birthday cake book. That year I chose a plane-shaped cake that I thought looked like a Spitfire.

Mum laughed and said, 'But you chose that last year.'

'I know that…but can I have it again this year…pleeeez?'

Mum smiled, gave me a gentle shove on the shoulder and said, 'One day, Johnny, you'll fly real planes like the models hanging around your bedroom.'

My younger brothers, Tommy, Mike and Andy, were nearly ready for school.

Mum, standing at the kitchen sink washing up the breakfast dishes, started on her usual preschool lectures: 'Button up your coats now. Make sure you stay together. Don't lose your lunch money. Look after each other.' Her dark, unruly hair was held tight in a silk scarf that she'd tied in a bow on the top of her head. A few curly tendrils had escaped to lie long and soft against her cheeks.

'She's saying the litany again,' Tommy whispered in my ear.

When Tommy learned a new word, he'd use it in every sentence until the next new one. 'I like the word litany,' he announced, and waited for us to say, 'Wow, Tom! You're a cracker with words.' But we didn't and he went on, 'It sounds soft like the touch of your tongue on your palate when you say it. I learned it in religious instruction, when we recited the Litany of the BVM.' (Palate had been his previous new word.).

'You're not supposed to say BVM,' I said.

'Why?' he asked, and I told him about the time Billy Scarfe got in terrible trouble the week before when he wrote 'Litany of BVM' in

"

an essay and old Miss Mullen made him write 'Blessed Virgin Mary' a hundred times on the blackboard.

Suddenly Mike said, 'Dad's coming.'

We rushed to pick up our school bags. Mum hadn't told us Dad had been out all night but we knew that when he came home unexpectedly in the morning like this, he'd be hungover and there'd be trouble. Mum turned from the sink. She stood holding a dishcloth that dripped water onto her apron, her shoes and the floor. I remember the look on her face. It was the same expression that Billy Scarfe got on his face when old Miss Mullen took the leather strap from her desk drawer and said, 'Come here, you.'

I'd just finished talking to Tommy when Dad barged in the door, slammed it shut and stood in the hallway snorting through flared nostrils. I saw the veins in his neck expand and purple. His eyes bulged and blazed in his face as if a fire burned in his head. The change from outside cold to inside warmth made his glasses steam up. He lost his balance and fell against the hall stand. The wellington boots, umbrellas, scarves and hats that were kept there fell in a tangle like a bunch of reptiles.

Mum said, 'Go on now, get to school,' and coaxed us towards the door.

Dad turned on her. 'What did you tell them?' he yelled, scrambling to his feet.

'I said, "Get to school",' she answered.

'I heard you say, "He's a fool!"'

'No. I said…'

He swung out and bashed Mum across the side of her face with his arm. She staggered back and grabbed the edge of the table. Breakfast plates, cups and cutlery shattered onto the floor. Dad charged towards Mum…head down, arms flailing like a bull lumbering towards a picador. My brothers nearly went hysterical. They knew that at times like this Dad would find some excuse to beat one of us with the razor strop that hung like the sword of Damocles on the handle of the kitchen door.

The drunken lout slipped on the wet floor then clutched the razor strop to pull himself up. Mum raised her head and I remember the dead dry look I saw in her eyes. My father came at her again.

I pushed myself between them and put my face right up to his so that our noses were nearly touching. With all the force of my ten-year-old lungs, I yelled, 'Leave her alone!'

'Don't, Johnny! Don't say anything more!' Mum screeched.

No one had ever dared challenge my father when he was on a rampage like this and for a split second he stood still. Then he grabbed me by the shoulders, shook me and threw me to the floor. I heard something snap and felt pain shoot through my body. Tommy, Mike and Andy made a circle around me. My father backed away and everything went black.

I don't remember much about the next few hours. Mum crying. A hospital. A plaster cast on my arm. I do remember that after the hospital, Mum took me and my brothers to the Royal Oak café, where we ate fruit flans and chocolate slices from a three-tier cake stand. My brothers autographed my stuccoed arm and we told knock-knock jokes to each other. Mum was quiet and kept looking into a space over our heads. When we left the restaurant, she took us to Grandma's place and left us there with a promise to come back before teatime.

Usually at Grandma's we played rummy or had a treasure hunt. But that day Grandma was very quiet and kept her lips pursed tight most of the time. She drew a happy face on my plastered arm and gave us fudge from a batch she'd made earlier. I got an extra piece for being brave.

We stayed at Grandma's for a long time before moving into a house a few doors down from her place and it became our habit to stop in to see her on our way home from school each day. She'd give us tumblers filled to the top with milk and when we had good news to tell her about our school work, she'd give us two of her home-made toffees. 'One for now and one for later,' she'd say. Sometimes we'd tell her fibs just to get the toffees.

Our new house wasn't as well furnished as our old one had been but it had a huge yard with lots of fruit trees. When the peaches and apricots and pears were in season, we'd help Mum prepare them for jam and preserves. A massive fig tree at the back of the yard grew the fattest figs I've ever seen. On summer mornings before we left for school, we'd make bets on which figs would ripen during the day.

Before Dad went off the rails, Mum used to sing as she went about her day and I remember the first time I heard her singing in the new house. She stood fussing with laundry from the line, folding sheets, shirts and underwear into separate piles for each of us. I remember watching her face as she sang, 'Try to remember a kind of September… When you were a tender and callow fellow…'

Parcels of comic books, chocolate or new jumpers started to arrive from Dad. I'd let my brothers share the surprises amongst themselves and slink into a corner. I never ate the chocolate or read the comic books no matter how much coaxing from my brothers. At these times, the old pain in my arm would spread to my chest and through my whole body and stay there until I'd kicked a football furiously around the oval for a long, long time.

Occasionally, he sent invitations to athletic events or horse trials and when he came to collect Tommy, Mike and Andy, he'd wait in the street and he'd be dressed in a suit and tie and look scrubbed clean. I'd want to ask him to help me build my latest model plane. Instead, I hid in my room. I never cried. Tommy told me that Dad kept looking back as if he was hoping I'd come tearing down the street after them but I never did. After a while, they stopped mentioning him while I was around.

Now and again when I had trouble getting to sleep, I'd take my mind back to a time when I'd watched Dad sharpen his open razor on the strop and he'd let me watch him shave. Back then, he and I would share breakfast and he'd teach me things like tying sheepshank knots and sometimes, before he left for work, he'd give me one of his old ties. We'd stand together, in front of the hall mirror, while I attempted to copy his Windsor knot. I don't remember when his drinking started or when the razor strop became a thing to fear.

Contact between the boys and my father dwindled to birthday and Christmas cards and by the time we had left college and started careers, that too had stopped.

When we were in our forties, and Grandma was ninety years old, Mum died from cancer. Sometimes towards the end of her life, she and I would sit on the veranda with a pot of tea between us and she'd ask me about my life as a pilot. Once, when she was in a melancholy mood, she told me that in their early years together my father took her dancing and on weekends they'd walk for hours around the countryside and talk about the life they'd build together. Most of our conversations were about her boys, especially Tommy – she seemed to worry more about him than her other three sons. Sometimes she'd start to sing one of her old songs and I'd coax the lyrics out of her paper-thin voice. I think she died of a broken heart.

Dad's drinking didn't start until after Tommy and I were born. Mum discovered then that Dad's father had been an alcoholic.

When the four of us got together to arrange her funeral we bragged about our successful careers, compared our latest cars, talked about technological advances and shared information about football, politics and the economy. Never in any discussion with me did my brothers talk about our father but I understood from overheard conversations between them that none of them knew where he was or whether he was still living in a drunken stupor.

While I built a career in the air force, Mike worked in computer technology and Andy in farming; Tommy's love for words took him to a career in journalism. Eventually he became an internationally recognised etymologist. I had many postcards he'd sent me from distant places early in his career. Sometimes there'd only be three of four words, like 'frisson', 'susurrus' 'penumbra', and a challenge for me to use them in my next letter or email to him.

When Andy poured drinks at Mum's wake, Tommy accused him

of being exiguous – and they argued for about ten minutes about the proper use of the word. Andy accepted Tommy's judgement and refilled his glass. I noticed his eagerness to get back to the bottle of Scotch and how his hands shook as he poured a third and fourth drink while Andy and Mike were still on their first.

Tommy derided me for sticking to soda water. 'Lighten up…get a life, Johnny,' he said, taking me by the elbow to the drinks corner.

Time and distance separated the four of us again until we were called to our dying father by nursing home staff. Tommy didn't come. He made excuses about work commitments but Mike told me Tommy's wife had left him because of his drunkenness and he was now living in a one-bedroom flat above an Irish pub in Boston.

*

Today, I stand at my father's bed looking at his decrepit body, remembering a time when he had stood tall above me. Then, he was a handsome man with clear wide eyes and a moustache the same colour as his bushy, dark hair. I see myself as a four- or five-year-old watching him snip and trim the edges until it was pencil thin. Now, I notice only straggled wisps of white hair on his top lip.

As I watch his powerless body, the slapping, slipping sound of a steel blade against leather comes clear and clean through distance and time to where I now stand beside him.

His room is bare. There are no hints of how he has spent the last bit of his life. Tiered shelves near the window, where other residents keep their books, magazines and music, are empty. Nothing hangs from the picture hooks that dot the walls. There is a bed, a small table with a lamp and a sheepskin-lined recliner chair where he lies during daytime hours. The only sound besides his stertorous breathing is the pulsing throb of an oxygen machine half-hidden under the table.

His head lolls to one side and his tongue falls over his bottom lip. It makes a perfect channel for saliva that trickles over his chin, seeps onto a bib or dribbles down the creases of withered skin around his neck. He doesn't seem to notice while strangers wash his hidden places and spoon feed him slushy nourishment.

The stink of incontinence repulses me and I struggle to stop myself vomiting. His hands and legs twitch and tremble and it seems to me that the essence of life is itching to get out of his rotting frame. He has lost the power of clear speech and now is only capable of gibbering incoherence. The noises that come from his mouth are those of a pig grunting, so different from a time when his voice had boomed curses and threats at us while we cowered in corners.

The arms that he'd used to batter my mother are splinted and wrapped in padded cotton sleeves. This protects him from bruising and I am reminded of a time when we'd be wakened in the night by his ranting and the sound of furniture being smashed and Mum sobbing behind the locked bathroom door. Next morning, she'd try to hide the contusions on her arms and face and we'd hear her tell Mrs Morgan, our next-door neighbour, she'd fallen in the darkened night hallway. I'm choked with memories.

An envelope sits against the lamp. After minutes of slurring and slavering, and with the help of a kindly nurse, I finally understand that my father wants me to have it. The 'Johnny' scrawled across the front made me wonder how he'd managed to write with hands that shook so badly…why me and not Tommy, Mike or Andy? I learn that he'd written the letter a few weeks before moving into the nursing home, when he still had some control of his hands.

I read it twice. The phrases 'truly sorry'; 'ashamed'; 'tried so hard'; 'couldn't stop'; 'forgive me' should stir compassion in me for this broken shell of a person. I feel nothing.

I try to distinguish the man I'd known from the form lying prone before me. I think about the lines Dylan Thomas wrote to his dying father:

Do not go gentle into that good night, rage, rage against the dying of the light.

Rage? Rage would be healthier than this numb nothing nothingness. I want to feel anger. I want to feel love. But ice keeps a lock on my heart.

In the mirror mounted on the back of the room door, I see my stony face looking back at me and realise it is the image of my father's younger face. While I stand there, a nurse comes in to check the bandages and move him from one side to the other. I look at the yellowed thick finger nails of his right hand. I pick it up…hold it for a few seconds.

His eyes open. He says, 'Johnny,' and the sound is like his old, young voice.

When the nurse finishes, she hands me a cardboard box about the size of a child's lunch box. 'This is all the personal items he had besides his clothes. I don't know if it's important to you but I didn't want to throw it away.'

I take it from her, close the door and hurry to my car, where I sit with the engine running, unable to slide the gears into drive. Among his pathetic belongings, I find a worn leather wallet. Inside, under a clear plastic cover, a photo dated the year I was born shows a young couple sitting on a park bench looking like they were glued together. They are laughing into the camera. I stare at the images for a long time and find it hard to believe that my parents had once been so young, so beautiful, so in love. I take the picture from his wallet and put it in mine. There is a small tattered notebook like the kind you keep in your shirt pocket to jot memos into. The tiny book has pages filled with addresses, dates and contact numbers that I'd used over the years and a list of my progression through the ranks of the air force. Initially the writing is strong and cursive but it becomes a spidery scrawl on the final pages. I touch the pages that his hands had touched…pages that mapped my life. I wish I'd asked him the questions that now spiral and spurt around in my head.

The phone calls I need to make can wait a while. I feel grateful for the rain that batters the windows and the noise of the engine running that covers my retching sobbing teeth-grinding shoulder-heaving grief.

I am besieged with a sudden urge to contact Tommy…spend time with him…talk to him about our father's legacy.

Charlie and me

Today, standing at the side of the house watching for Charlie, I remember the wide glowing grins that used to sweep across his face. Smiles that now hide behind a mask as if he is some sad stranger.

He's later than usual. I spend the waiting time scanning an ancient willow tree where shoots of new life lurk between branches, low and heavy, sweeping the lawn like a housewife expecting company. From somewhere close by, a whiff of jasmine floats past my nose to remind me...of...? I clamp my eyes tight shut and turn my head away, the way you do at the scary bits of a murder movie.

I heard the slap and scratch of leather on the footpath – left, right, left, right – and watched Charlie turn the corner at the end of our street. His head drooped. His chin rested on his chest. His sports bag barely cleared the surface of the paving stones and his socks were scrunched around his ankles like a knitted concertina.

Yesterday, when I'd stood at the front gate watching for him, I'd noticed the flick of a lace curtain and the flash of a face in a bay window of the house next door – same as today before I moved to the side of the house. I'd seen the middle-aged couple that lived there working in an aviary at the back of their garden. Sometimes I'd seen the old man on his knees weeding around a flower bed at our adjoining fence. Once, I tried to catch his eye and almost called out 'Hello' but the greeting stayed tucked up in my throat like a tight parcel of stone.

Since our arrival in the village, at unguarded moments incessant shifting patterns of fear and guilt grab my heart and clench it tight. At times like that, I force myself to remember the last time I laughed. How many lifetimes?

Charlie came through the gate, marched past me and charged in the front door.

I said, 'Hi, Charlie!'

He threw his backpack and sports bag in a corner in the hallway before fleeing to the other end of the house. The slap of his feet on tiles echoed through the half empty house. Today was his third day at the village school and each day he'd come home more miserable than the day before.

I tiptoed along the hallway and listened at his bedroom door. I raised curled fingers shoulder high, tapped on the door, called out, 'I'm coming in,' and turned the door knob.

He crouched on the floor with his back against the foot of his bed. His arms curled tight around his legs and his head rested on his knees. He looked up, and I could see tears the size of a five-cent piece ready to burst from the corners of his eyes. A calendar and black felt-tipped pen lay beside him on the floor. I picked them up and hunkered down to his level. Every date since we'd been left on our own had been blacked out.

'Charlie…Charlie, I know it's tough for you and I'm not sure if coming here was the best choice, but we…please…take a long deep breath and look at me…talk to me!'

'I hate that school. I'm never going back,' he mumbled.

'What happened today?'

'It's just that…just everything! I miss my room and my stuff. Nobody talks to me…I…I miss Dad.'

'Charlie, I know…I know you're hurting. I know 'cos I'm hurting too. I know it's hard to face our troubles. I don't know what else to say to you.' I put the calendar and pen aside and settled down on the floor beside him.

He didn't pull away from me when I started stroking his head. I whispered in his ear, 'Charlie, remember what your father used to say: "If you think you can or you think you can't, you're probably right." Remember?'

'Hm, sure, Ma...but...'

'Charlie, pretty soon we'll find a friend or two, I'll get a job and the money situation will sort itself out and we'll get everything we need in time.'

'Yeah, Mum, I know, but I've got assignments that need to be done by next week! What can I do without a computer? All the kids at school have their own laptops and iPods and they can do really cool work and...' He gulped and punched the floor with two clenched fists.

I reached over and nudged at a stray curl on his forehead. The sun, shining through the long window in front of us, glinted on his jet black hair, blessing him with tiny lambent stars. When the light began to fade, I uncurled my cramped legs and kissed the top of his head.

'Time to start cooking...it's your favourite chicken dish tonight,' I coaxed.

A wan smile appeared at the corner of his mouth.

While I chopped carrots and beans, Charlie told me about his homework project.

'We have to write five hundred words about some aspect of nature and we have to include photos or drawings. And we have to list where we did our research — like a bibli...bibliogr...'

'Bibliography?'

'Yeah, that's it.'

'Great practice that, for when you get to high school.'

Next morning, I walked with Charlie as far as the street that led to the school. He didn't complain. I watched and waited until he'd gone through the main gate. I saw him walking through little groups of pupils congregating here and there in the yard. I thought I heard laughter coming from one particular group and my body froze into a life-size icicle. Only my tight straight lips held my lurching heart inside my body as I walked on in the direction of the supermarket.

When I turned into the breakfast cereal aisle, I spotted my next-door neighbours. The man was trying to dislodge a packet of oatmeal from the top shelf.

I took a deep breath and said, 'Can I help you?'

Just then, the box dislodged and fell on my head. I stumbled back but managed to grab it an instant before it would've landed on the floor.

The woman clapped both hands to her chubby face, uttering in a loud whisper, 'Oh, my goodness, Joe, you nearly knocka outa the woman! I tol' you it was too higha for a you to reach.' She turned to me. 'Oh! oh! You is the neighbour woman. The leetle boy's mama. I am so pleased to introduce us here.' Her voice grew louder, her eyes flashed and her hands, decorated with gold rings and bangles, waved in the air. She stuck out a hand. 'My name Isabella, you call me Bella! Dis here clumsy person is my husband Giuseppe – you call him Joe. Pliz, I'm sorry you got hit.'

Shoppers, amused at the kerfuffle, made wide paths around us.

'Okay, Bella…it's me to apologise.' The man turned to face me, saying in a voice that reminded me of thick, soft velvet, 'I am an oaf. You hurt?'

A giggle leapt from my mouth and I felt a smile separate my scrunched-up lips. I put the purchase in their trolley. 'No, I'm fine, really.' I offered my hand. 'I'm Helen Larkin.'

'Tell me,' Bella said, 'whatsa matter your son yesday? I watch him – he no' happy boy. How's he doin' school?, I vexed to see him come home, he look forlorn. I want to give him big fat hug.'

Joe piped up, 'You wanna give hug to everone, Bella.'

'Ah, you jus' jealous 'cos you wan' all my attention!' Bella laughed through her words.

We chatted while navigating our trolleys through passages stacked with sauces and cleaning materials and dairy produce. It was agreed that we'd walk together for the ten-minute stroll home, each carrying a bag of shopping.

When we'd nearly reached their cottage, I saw Joe nudge Bella. She looked at him, her eyebrows knitted together.

He nodded towards their house then a sideways nod to me,

'Ah! I know what you tryin' tell me,' Bella said. 'Helen, woulda you like for a cup of coffee? It'sa the bes' coffee in town. An' lovely cake jus' waitin' for you – you too skinny!'

'Thanks, I'd love to.'

While Bella busied herself with coffee pot, cups and plates, Joe asked me how I liked living in the village.

'Well, it's hard to say at this point. We've been here only two weeks and Charlie isn't very happy at school.'

'I hopa he no' bein' bullied,' Bella interrupted from behind me.

'No, it's not so much that, it's that he misses…his…fa…friends. He's worried about homework assignments. We can't afford a computer yet.'

'Where's his papa? Why you come here?'

Joe, drumming his fingers on the table and staring out the window interrupted. 'Wha' dis assignment 'bout?'

I repeated the outline Charlie had given me.

''Member, Bella…'member what it like wen we firs coma 'ere?'

'Sure I do,' Bella answered, placing slabs of chocolate cake and dollops of cream on small white plates. 'We had four babies in dis house an' they all sleep in same bed…an' no one speak to us at first. We didn' talka English for a longa time…at leas' you 'ave the language.'

I nodded.

She went on, 'You so lucky to have such a good-lookin' boy still beside you. My sons all gone now. An' my girl, Angela. They all married. We have six beautiful grandchildren…they all coming dis weekend. You come in Sunday an' we have lunch.'

Joe pushed his plate aside. 'I got a idea. How old you say Charlie is?'

'Nine. He'll be ten in six months.'

'Same age my grandson Joe. He's a computer genius…you bring Charlie on Sunday and Joe will help him. An' another ting, I gotta heaps of photos and mag'zines on pigeons an' how to breed dem. In fac', you bring Charlie in tonight an' he can use my computer an' we have a nice talk about nature an' birds.'

By the time I'd left them, I knew all about the hardships of their early migrant life and learned the names of their children and grandchildren. Sharing time with Bella and Joe in their world of colour and comfort was like slipping into a clean warm bed on a cold winter night.

That evening after dinner, I introduced Charlie to our new friends. While Bella and I talked recipes in the kitchen, Joe asked Charlie to help him Google for information about nesting boxes. As they marched off to the study at the back of the house, I suspected Joe already knew everything there was to know about the subject.

Early on Saturday morning, Charlie actually bounced out of bed and raced to the kitchen. He hopped from one foot to the other and a spark bounced in his eyes. 'I'm to be next door in five minutes.' He slurped through mouthfuls of corn flakes.

'You're smiling, Charlie.'

'Yeah!'

Two minutes later, I watched him barge down next-door's path with a bundle of jotters and loose papers under his arm. He hadn't taken the time to tie his shoelaces or comb his hair.

By noon, I decided he'd been there long enough. Bella was in the kitchen cooking for Sunday's lunch. She waved her arms, pointed at bowls and platters spread along bench tops, and in her laughing loud and warm voice she rattled off a litany, 'Rigatoni, *farfalle*, *pasta e ravioli*.'

The names meant little to me but the aromas made me drool like a half-starved waif. Flamboyant ceramic bowls and platters filled shelves, crystal sparkled behind glass. In this house of meticulous radiance, I felt blest with feelings of belonging.

'We no' need young Joe to help,' Joe senior announced when he and Charlie trooped back into the kitchen. 'Dis one a here teached me everting I need.'

Charlie looked up to Joe the way a devotee would look if their god arrived, live, at their side.

At the door, as we were leaving, Joe ruffled his hair. 'See you t'morrow. Don' forget to bring your project. I wanna see the finish.'

My heart soared as we scuttled home and Charlie prattled on about his experience. 'You should see the pigeons, Mum! There's hundreds of them… The bird house is called a loft and a group of pigeons is called a kit and Joe takes them fifty miles away and they find their way back home!'

'It's Mr Scapinello, Charlie.'

'No…Joe says it's okay to call him Joe. I've had such a great time… what's for lunch?'

Charlie spent the afternoon cutting and pasting paragraphs and photos into an art portfolio and before he went to bed he showed me the results of his labour. He'd described the feeding and breeding habits of birds and how each bird had a band put on its leg when only a few days old and he imitated the way Joe whistled and cooed to them.

On Sunday, Bella and Joe set up a long table on the back veranda. Gleaming white linen was covered by pasta dishes separated by huge bowls of chicken and beef, sauces, salads, bread sticks, focaccia, cheeses, antipasti and carafes of wine the colour of ripe plums. It was a day of introductions, music, loud conversations and invitations. And through it all, miracles tumbled together in a prism of possibilities. I learned that Bella's daughter Angela owned a staff recruitment business. She booked me in for an interview the following morning and assured me that I'd have a job soon.

Charlie and young Joe found a corner to talk football and computer games.

Later, when everyone had gone, I stayed behind to help Bella clear up and put things away while Charlie and Joe split the time between the pigeon loft and the study.

'Wha's you story, Helen?' she asked above the rattle of bottles and plates. 'Where you come from? I see sadness in you face. Tell me 'bout Charlie's father.'

'Yes, the past months have been hard on us…our house…' I wanted to spread my hard-packed miserable thoughts out like a tablecloth. I wanted to see how they'd look when turned into words, but just then I heard Charlie's laugh coming from the study, accompanied by a loud guffaw from Joe.

Suddenly, I didn't want to disturb the peace of this wonderful happy place. It was too soon to tell Bella about the fire that had swallowed my beloved Thomas and claimed everything we owned. Talking about these things could wait. It was enough for now to have found a healing corner where Charlie and I could learn to laugh again.

Disinherited

Great Aunt Ethel's annual visit is imminent and our household is in an agitated state. Everything has been cleaned: windows, carpets, floors burnished. Frances and I are ejected from the guest room and, with our clothes and games, relocated to Millie's room at the end of the hall. We don't mind this too much 'cos we get to eavesdrop on Millie's phone calls to her latest boyfriend and experiment with her bags of make-up when she isn't looking. She hates us.

Every five minutes, Mum is shouting instructions. 'Frances, find yon pink dress I made for you. It needs the hem fixed.' Or 'Millie, if you don't want those two using your foundation and lipstick, put them away where they can't find them… C'mon, get a move on. We'll be late for the airport!'

Great Aunt Ethel is only about a hundred and fifty centimetres in height but nearly that in rotundity. She only wears black or brown and rarely smiles. It's hard to tell the colour of her eyes and hair due to a fatty face and silly hats. Mum says she's an ancient replica of old Margaret Rutherford, the famous character actor. Ethel asks us questions about school and what do we think of the economic situation. The first time she asked that, Frances and I sniggered and fidgeted and Mum got real mad.

So we pile into the car, leaving the front passenger seat vacant for Eth. We argue all the way to the airport about who gets to sit beside her at dinner. Nobody wants the honour 'cos auntie smells like a public loo – especially when she's been enclosed in a jet for the three-hour flight.

Mum gives us the usual lecture about behaviour. 'Be nice to Ethel. She's getting very old.'

'Why does she have to come to us anyway?' Fran asks.

'Because we're the next best thing she has to a family,' Mum answers.

'It's almost summer. I hope she's not wearing that awful fur coat.' That's Millie, the fashion queen.

'Prob'ly is,' I say. 'I think it's the only one she's got.'

We wait behind the barrier, watching doors swing open and shut and people hugging and kissing each other. Ethel is one of the first to come through – pushed in a wheelchair by a flight attendant. She's wearing a bashed felt hat that meets her eyebrows and has an old wrinkled leather bag slung round her neck and resting on her belly. She's wrapped in a fur coat as big as our two-man tent and we can see the bare pelt of muskrats at places where the fur has been rubbed away. A wrinkled navy blue skirt reaches her ankles and I'm surprised it doesn't get caught up in the wheels.

Mum drags us with her eyes to do the polite greeting thing and we hover, waiting for the signal to give Ethel a peck on the cheek. Great Aunt Ethel speaks with a toffee accent. She was a schoolteacher a hundred years ago and says things like 'Children should be seen and not heard.' Can you believe that? Mum says if we mind our manners and do nice things for our visitor, she might leave all her money to us when she dies. We get Ethel and all her stuff into the car and she starts to tell us about her rheumatism and bursitis and how long she had to wait for attention at the airport. Frances holds her nose and mouths, 'Blah, blah, blah.' I giggle and Mum glares at us in the rear-view mirror.

We pull into our driveway. I shut the gate just before Murphy our border collie, charges round from the yard. We each give him a pat and ruffle his ears as he jumps from one to the other. When he sees Eth, he stops dead. His ears and tail flop and he backs off.

'It's okay, Murph,' Frances reassures him.

Millie takes Ethel's bags and coat and tells her, 'I'll put these in your room.'

Mum puts the kettle on and fills a plate with shortbread and fruit slices she'd made earlier. Frances and I go off for a swim.

We're doing laps and practising our tumble turns for the next swimming carnival when Fran shouts, 'Hey, what's Murphy up to?'

The silly dog is dragging something brown and furry along the edge at the far end of the pool. He's worrying at it and growling like he wants the thing to play with him. He gets in a real fankle. I'm just about to go and help him when he and the bundle go over the edge and end up flailing at the deep end. Murphy pops his head out from under Ethel's musquash coat as it slowly sinks to the bottom.

'Oh…my…gawd!' I call out to Fran, who can't stop laughing. 'Mum'll kill us…she'll send Murph to the vet for the big needle! You gotta help me, Fran.'

We push and pull and drag and great clumps of fur come away in our hands. We're struggling to get the hulk out of the water when Millie's head pokes out from the kitchen window.

'D'you two want…' Then, 'Mum, come quick! Muuuuum!'

Mum scurries out. Frances and I are breathless and hair from Ethel's coat is sticking to our arms and faces. Patches of floating fur dot the surface of the pool like thousands of squiggly dead worms. Murphy has a bout of sneezing as he tries to get rid of clinging muskrat by rubbing his body across the lawn.

Mum sits down with a thump. She sticks her feet in the pool. She looks at the shambles and starts to giggle. The four of us convulse with laughter.

'Well…I guess,' Mum hoots, 'we can say goodbye to our inheritance.'

Black borders

The truck had seen better days. Worn tyres, barely protected by dented rusted mudguards, managed to keep the chassis off the ground. The tray sides rattled in protest and a wet, black collie cowered in a corner on top of some rain-soaked sacks.

John Young, the farmer, puffed on his fourth cigarette for the day and cursed the weather and the war. 'Women,' he muttered. 'No' a muscle between them, no decent labour left.' He spat and shook as he steered the truck to a halt at the end of the street where the village began.

Fran Morgan stood huddled with a group of friends and neighbours in the grey morning mist. They were cold, wet and anxious about getting on the truck. It would ensure them a day's work for three shillings 'n' ninepence and whatever tomatoes or vegetables they could smuggle out in secret corners of their clothing. Some of the women wore dungarees with big pockets – dungarees that their husbands had swapped for uniforms of war.

Fran's dark, unruly curls were held in place by a red and green silk scarf. The pattern was oriental and it was tied neatly in a bow at the top of her forehead.

'I like your scarf, Fran,' Belle Johnson said.

'Thanks, Belle. Have you heard from Jimmy yet?'

'No, Fran, but no news is good news.'

The small talk was interrupted by farmer Young. 'How many of ye know how to pick rhubarb?'

All the hands went up.

'How many of ye know how to pick tomatoes?'

Again all the hands went up.

'Right then, I'll expect all of you to give a good day's work for a day's pay. Any o' ye caught stealin' the produce get fired on the spot and you find your own way home. Right then, in the truck wi' ye.'

The women giggled and whispered excitedly as they scrambled onto the mudguards and over the sides. Mary Gallacher's rubber-soled shoes wouldn't keep still on the metal truck floor, causing gales of laughter as she slithered and grabbed for an arm or a jacket to steady herself. Finally, she sat down with a thud and a yelp of protest from the collie, who nursed his bruised tail for the rest of the journey.

The truck trundled on over the hills past the local sawmill and the sewage plant.

When the sun filtered through the clouds, melting the morning mist, the women started singing. A rousing rendition of 'Keep right on to the end of the road' was their theme song.

It was April 1942 and while the men of the village were fighting for survival on the Western front, Malayan jungles and prison camps, the women struggled to provide food for their families. Their war involved taking any opportunities to earn a little money and to find food that didn't use up their precious ration coupons. People like Grumpy Young were a godsend to them.

Young gave each of the women an area to work while once more reinforcing his rules. 'You – Morgan! Work over in the forcing shed and don't step on the young plants.'

Fran had been looking at the scenery around her, listening to the sound of birdsong, smelling the deep rich fecund smell of ploughed earth and was startled and embarrassed. She hadn't a clue what she was supposed to do but she moved towards the building anyway.

Beyond the sheds and farm buildings, a serrated line of hills met the sky. On summer Sundays before the war, Fran and Terry had taken the children on long hikes through these hills. Sometimes they'd carry cans and fill them with ripe, fat blackberries. Or the children would gather great bags of rose hips and sell them in the next town for sixpence a bag. She looked to the sky, hoping the breeze would catch her thoughts and fly them through the ether to her man. The last time she'd heard from Terry was six months ago when he'd sent her the silk scarf. She knew it was from Singapore.

Mary Gallagher caught her eye. 'It's okay, Fran. It's dead easy. All you do is pluck the young stems of rhubarb, cut off the leaves and put them on the pallets of straw. Somebody else'll pick them up.'

'Thanks, Mary. I'll see you at lunchtime.' She tied her sackcloth apron around her waist.

'Fran, I almost forgot! You have to work by candlelight. The shed's pitch black. Strong sunlight's bad for the plants. The candles are in holders at the door of the shed.'

'Do you know, this rhubarb goes to France to make wine?' Mary Gallagher told them as they sat around eating their lunch in the shade of a barn door.

'How can they be makin' wine in France when there's a war on?' Kath Wilson asked.

'I don't know, but that's what I've been told,' Mary said, munching her way through bread and cheese.

The morning had gone well for Fran. She'd adjusted to the dark, working up and down the rows of the delicate plants. They feel almost like sticks of silk, she thought, placing them on pallets of hay. She was quite happy to work on her own. It was peaceful. No one interrupted her with idle chatter and it gave her an opportunity to think about her children and Terry. 'I hope Peter got them off to school on time. And I hope Missy remembered to wear the dress I ironed for her.'

When farmer Young called to her at lunchtime, he nearly complimented her when he saw her tally. 'That's no' bad for a woman,' he said. 'Can ye come back tomorrow?'

'Yes,' Fran answered, through clenched teeth.

They'd started work at seven that morning. By three in the afternoon, backs and legs were aching, fingers were sore and raw from the tedious routine. It was a great relief to hear Young's whistle signalling the end of the day.

Fran wanted to be home before the children returned from school. She was first on the truck. 'Thank God that's over,' she said to Kath Wilson as they settled in the truck trying not to damage their loot of tomatoes and rhubarb.

They didn't speak much on the way home. They were preoccupied with their separate situations at home.

As the truck neared the drop-off point, Mary Gallagher shouted, 'Look, it's Thompson the postie!'

The village postman regularly cycled through the streets with his little leather despatch bag slung across his body. At nine in the morning and two in the afternoon, no one paid much attention. But at other hours people knew it was a telegram.

'Who is it this time?' they whispered, their eyes following his direction.

Sometimes it would be good news; someone posted as missing in action had been found safe. But most often these days, he delivered a black-bordered symbol of sadness and grief and the women of the village would rally to support and comfort the weeping mother or wife. All eyes turned to see where he'd come from. His big black bike, oblivious to its significance, carried him on. The women looked at each other. Nobody spoke.

Fran saw Peter and Missy walking towards the truck and wondered why they were home so early. They were solemn and slow. Mary Gallagher and Kath Wilson moved to either side of her. They knew they'd be needed before they saw the black-bordered missive Peter brought from his pocket.

Foxy ladies

We slowed down to Grandma's speed as she wobbled along the corridor rattling out instructions as we moved.

'Be sure to give those tapestries to the names I've put on the back… I've stuck notes on bits of furniture about how I want them disposed of…and remember Oscar likes his milk slightly warmed.'

We'd decided to keep Oscar, her twelve-year-old cat…we'd bring him to her now and again for a visit. I watched her watching our car move down the curve of the driveway. She leant against a brick wall and waved a cheerio with her walking stick. I felt vexed for this frail old soul who'd been such a godsend to me when Emma and Jack were little.

Tom and I have taken on the job of cleaning out her house to get it ready for the real estate market and it's mid-morning when we arrive at the old place. Emma and her current lover, Toby, are in the yard picking the last of that season's apricots. Their shoes are stained with blobs of rotting fruit and Emma's chin glints with strings of yellow juice.

Grandpa had been a builder-handyman and he'd extended the house backwards, sidewards and upwards with whatever bricks, tiles and timber he'd snaffled over the years from sites he'd worked on. The result is a bigger, uglier model of the Ettamogah Pub. There is no unity in the shape of it. Inside, the odd-shaped rooms with unexpected corners are full of ancient furniture. Lamps and ornaments sit on crocheted doilies and rickety beds are covered in patchwork quilts.

'C'mon, you two,' Tom calls out. 'Time to get started. Emma, you take the cupboard under the stairs and put everything out on the back porch.'

'I want Toby to help me.'

'No way! You and he would get nothin' done. He's comin' up in the loft wi' me.'

Emma, arms folded across her body, glares at Tom's back. I move into the kitchen and I can hear thumps and thuds coming from the hallway as she spews her anger over the dusty detritus.

I'm writing out lists of things to be sold, things to take to the Salvos, things to give away, when her scream just about raises the old roof. Before I can put my pen down, she barrels white and jittery into the kitchen. I race double time to where she points, one arm stretched and shaking in front of her. A heap of fur, with two green eyes and a hard black snout at one end, lies half in and half out the cupboard door.

'It bit me! It bit me!' Emma yells, flailing her arms, at the same time giving her face close inspection in the hall mirror.

'Don't be silly, Emma, that thing's been dead for nearly a hundred years – if it ever had a bite in it, there's none left now.'

Tom and Toby dash down from the loft.

'What's the drama?' Tom asks, pushing in front of Toby.

I pick up the offending hunk of fur. Emma, eyes bulging and shoulders hunched, stands a few feet away.

'It's a fox fur, Emma…used to be fashionable in the forties.'

'You mean people actually wore real, dead foxes?'

'Sure did.' I drape the dead animal over my shoulders. I clip the head to the tail and twirl around. 'Look, see how flattering fur is.'

Emma spits a loud 'Yeugh!'

She takes Toby's hand, and both move sideways down the hall, out the door to the back garden. Tom cackles and starts rummaging where Emma had left off. Battered boxes appear from the cavity and I hear him scuffling around like a dog worrying a bone. I stand stroking the fur, trying to picture Gran wearing it over shimmering satin. Backless bottle green? Drapes of ivory? Perhaps deep burgundy? But an image of her bowed body and shaking hands blots out my musings.

'Put the kettle on,' Tom calls out.

I pour two mugs of coffee and open a tin of biscuits.

He trudges into the kitchen brushing dust and cobwebs from his hair. 'Didn't know we're dressing for morning tea,' he quips, tickling the fox's head. 'You must be melting in that thing.'

'Y'know, it's hard to believe that Gran was once a young woman going off to dances with shiny hair and eyes and dolled up in satin and fur…maybe I should take this to her…get her to talk about her young days.'

'Good idea,' Tom says, stirring sugar into his coffee.

Gran is sitting on a bench under a liquidambar tree when I arrive. Her eyes are closed and her hands lie still in her lap. Her old linen gardening hat, tilted sideways, shelters her face from the glare of the setting sun.

'Hello, Meggie. I'm so glad to see you,' she says without opening her eyes.

'How'd you know it was me?' I ask.

She laughs. 'Well, you have the same footstep as your mother. Shirley never walked. She thumped along like she was on a mission to put the world to rights, just like you do.' She opens her eyes when I put the bundle in her lap. She peers over her glasses and lets out the heartiest laugh. 'Well, I never! Where in heaven's name did this pop up from?'

'Emma found it under the stairs. She thought it was alive!'

'More than I can say for that creature she's seeing.' Gran chortles and sniffs at the fur. 'Albert bought this for me on our first anniversary.'

'When was the last time you wore it?' I ask.

She smiles and closes her eyes.

I wait.

'Let me see now. Yes…it was our tenth wedding anniversary…we were going out to a dinner dance at the RSL. Your mother would've been about eight and for a dress-up treat I let her wear the fox while I finished doing my hair. She pranced and whirled in front of the mirror.

Then she stroked the fur as if it was a pet rabbit. Shirley didn't want to let it go. I remember how we laughed…like people do when they're young and in love with the world. That's my favourite memory of your mother.'

Gran's lips quiver and she stuffs the relic back into the plastic bag. 'Albert and I had a great time but, y'know, the fashion changed and the old thing was put away…never saw it again until now.'

I help her to her feet and we make our way to the common lounge room, where a few residents are watching television. She settles in a seat and shows her treasure to two nearby women.

A woman, Maxine, sitting nearest Gran, picks it up and drapes it over her shoulders. She pulls her thinning hair over one eye, picks up a pencil and, holding it between her right index finger and middle finger, she pouts and poses like an ad for cigarettes. Then she totters up and down bowing now and again to giggles and quiet applause from her audience.

One old dear says she's got copies of plays and maybe they should start a drama group. Someone else says they'd been a director in one of the bigger theatre groups in the city and could still get access to any props they might need.

A male voice pipes up. 'If you like, I'll design programs on my computer.'

Another tells about a time when he'd played the lead in Eugene O'Neill's *Long Day's Journey Into Night*. 'So if you need a male voice, count me in.'

Eyes brighten and energy gathers speed as suggestions are mooted across the floor from wheelchairs and Zimmer frames.

I stroke Gran's back and smooth wayward strands of hair from her face. I say, 'Cheerio,' but my voice gets lost amongst the babble.

The fox fur straddles the back of a chair and no one notices as I close the door of the common room quietly behind me.

Imagination

I'm sitting in the dentist's waiting room trying to take my mind off imminent root canal work by idly leafing through a *Home Beautiful* magazine. Articles on 'Making Use of Space' or 'Bathroom Renovations on a Budget' float past; text and images meld into the background of my mind like advertisements on the side of a passing bus.

I'm just about to turn another page when I see it. Just like that! There, on page forty-six…a picture of the first house I remember living in. The peeling paint and tarnished brass fittings on the front door have been restored and the house is surrounded by lawns shorn as neat as putting greens on a golf course. Borders built by shrubbery, a herb garden and rose beds glisten on the page. Now, the oak panels on the door look like burnished bronze. They seem to be calling a welcome to me. I trace my fingers up, down and around its glossy frame, close my eyes and let recollections of times past surge and flow around me.

I opened the door, sidled into the hallway and stopped a few steps in at the kitchen door on the left to see my mother as she'd looked in my childhood. She stood tall and slim by the sink, sleeves rolled up past her elbows, piling up washed baking tins on the draining board to her right. Her dark curls were tied up in a colourful scarf with some mischievous tendrils escaping to frame her pale face. Wire trays with fresh-baked loaves sat on a table near an open window and the smell of their freshness tumbled back through the years and made me salivate. The living room, to the right of the kitchen, was where we spent winter evenings playing board games and reading and where sometimes in the morning, lines of dust motes could be seen stretching from mullioned windows onto surfaces of cluttered furniture.

Five doors on each side of the long linoleum-covered passageway that trailed beyond the entrance had our names printed on sticky paper. But the aged sticker on the door of the last room on the left at the end of the lobby was labelled the Empty Room. No one slept there.

The truth is, the empty room was full to the ceiling with remnants, rejects, cast-offs and junk that had been thrown into the corners because we didn't know where else to put the fragments of our disordered life. This room was so full of great stuff that we often called it the Glory Hole.

An observer could read our family's social history by a quick look around this refuge. Tents and poles, groundsheets, water bags, a primus stove, and torches. Tackle boxes, fishing rods and waders. Bikes and bike parts lay beside punctured tubes and tyres. Boxes and bags overflowed with georgette, calico, tweed and velvet superseded fashions. Flapper dresses from the twenties snuggled into knee-length skirts and shoulder-padded jackets from the forties. Piles of books in the corners were stacked beside boxes of magazines and past issues of *The Wizard*, *Boys Own*, *Girls Own*, and the *Dandy* and *Beano* comic books. And there, in a corner, was a three-wheeled doll's pram beside a doll's house with a hole in the roof where Moses, our kitten, would peek at us through green cellophane windows.

It seemed that things were always disappearing in our house. We never knew where our belongings had gone.

When one of the boys asked, 'Where's my cricket bat?' Mum, shrugging as she bent over sink or stove, would answer, 'Och, it's likely to be in the Empty Room.'

'Where's my lunch?' or 'Where's my white socks?' from one of the girls got the same response.

Sometimes, wanting to test whether Mum was listening or not, one of us would ask a question while the others giggled and smirked behind her, moving our mouths to mimic her predictable answer.

She'd turn round real fast like a whippet after a rabbit, laughing and saying, 'I ken what you lot are up to,' and she'd pretend to swipe us with whatever she had in her hand (usually a tea towel or a wooden spoon). Poor Mum, trying to keep ten feral children in order was a task far beyond her energy levels.

On dreich days, when the rain was fine and soft, she'd send us to the Empty Room to tidy things up. But our idea of putting things in order was having a dress-up party and we'd start with the boxes and bags of old clothes.

One typical day, my twin sister Chrissie and I dressed to the nines trying to imitate glamorous women we'd seen in movie magazines. I teamed a moth-eaten fox fur with a silver-grey satin backless dress that fell in folds at my ankles and trailed two feet behind me. Elbow-length white gloves with about twenty buttons reached to my shoulders. And on my head, a brown cloche hat with a faded silk rose fastened on its rim.

'The hat doesn't go wi' the dress,' Chrissie said.

'But I like the hat…it feels soft…and I like the rose…see, the green leaves match okay. I feel like a queen.'

'Well, lah dee dah, I'd rather be dancing,' Chrissie spat back at me, pulling on a black pleated jitterbug skirt and a soft blue crepe de Chine blouse with wide shoulders. Then she needed my help to strap wedged-heel shoes with narrow bands of black patent leather around her ankles.

'Your shoes don't match, Chrissie, and you'll fall and break your neck if you try walking in them.' I said, seconds before she toppled onto a box of old curtains.

'Doesn't matter if the shoes match…they're pretty and elegant,' she taunted, struggling to her feet and flicking her hands down her front. 'Besides, they make me look tall and lanky.'

We slung every strand of colourful beads we could find around our necks and took on the posture of hunchbacks with the weight of them.

Chrissie never wore a hat for dress-ups. Her hair was thick, dark, auburn and lay in soft waves half-way down her back and settled over her left eye, in the style of Veronica Lake. My brothers sometimes called her Veronica Puddles and she'd toss her head and stomp across the room as if she was the star of some film.

The boys were supposed to sort out the piles of comic books and magazines but they spent their time cutting out images of Johnny Weissmuller or a spitfire plane, or the title page of a magazine showing a car or a Sherman tank. They attached these to the walls with cobbler's tacks or drawing pins.

Mum looked in now and again saying things like 'You'll be a fine artist one o' these days, Johnny,' or 'You look right bonnie in that dress, Jean. Green brings out the shine in your eyes.'

Chrissie preened in front of her asking, 'Who am I, Ma?'

'Och, you're a film star…can't mind the name but you look just like her – maybe even better looking,' and we laughed like children at a circus.

Sometimes, on fine days, we'd resurrect the old camping equipment and two small tents assembled in our yard became a tent city, an army camp, or perhaps an archaeological dig. We'd get our eldest brother Joe to help us print notices about particular activities. Something like

Archaeological Project.
Entry only to approved personnel.
Others – keep out!

Digging for prehistoric artefacts meant we had to stash them in secret places some time before the hunt. These treasures could be shards of pottery or broken china; perhaps a rabbit's foot or a tin of buttons. After they'd been found, we'd catalogue and classify them in jotters ruled and headed with columns describing the item, date, who found and where found. The digging left us with smudges of dirt on our faces, black under our fingernails and holes all over the yard.

During these imaginative escapades, it was a regular thing to name our younger siblings – Eric, Alfie, Cathy and Arthur – The Eejits and give them roles of refugees or maybe prisoners of war. We fed them crusts of dry bread and water and made them sit in a corner until ordered to a task. When Mum found out about this, she put us on the same rations and fed our victims some of her newly baked biscuits or apple cake.

Back then, the house was separated from Farmer Gibb's field by a picket fence which had flaky bits of white paint that waved about in a breeze and gaps here and there where slats should be, like the spaces left by missing teeth in an ancient mouth.

Once, Chrissie and I found our grandfather's spare set of false teeth; we put it in an empty polish tin and buried it in a corner of Gibb's cow patch. Eric told Mum, and in spite of cries 'It wasn't me… it was him/her!' or 'He/she made me do it!' we were sentenced to early bedtime and no pudding.

Our days in the Glory Hole came to an end one day with the news that Aunt Peggy, Uncle Frank and their two children were coming to live with us for a while. They had come home to Scotland from Canada for an extended holiday. When World War II broke out, they had to stay on our side of the Atlantic until it was safe to sail back to Canada. Waiting for the changes to our life was like having the sword of Damocles hanging from the ceiling of the Empty Room.

'So Ma…because of the war, we have to put up with Peggy?' Johnny asked.

'That's right, m'dearies. The inspector of works is comin' to check you all out. And it's Aunt Peggy – remember that,' Mum said, looking out of the nearest window into the distance and smiling. It was as if she could see the cavalry and wagons labelled 'RELIEF' galloping towards her.

'Aunt Peggy!' Chrissie snapped. 'She's too bossy and crabby…she'll have us cleanin' from mornin' till night. I'm tired just thinkin' about it.'

Peggy was my father's sister who'd spent many years in America and Canada as a housekeeper to wealthy families. She was a short roly-poly owl-like woman who wore a hairnet and aprons with large pockets as she bustled around glaring at us over her glasses. I knew she had a sense of humour because sometimes I'd catch her and Mum laughing over a cup of tea in the kitchen, but she never laughed with us.

Our favourite names for Peggy were Disinfectant Dinah (Dee Dee) or Commander in Chief (Cee Cee), used only when she and Mum were out of earshot. The Empty Room and another next to it were allocated to our visitors and the minute they arrived Peggy declared war.

'What in heaven's name is a bicycle doing in here? Take that out! Move those shoes! Make some space in here! Pick up this box! Find a container for the rubbish! Get those scraps of paper off the wall! Open these curtains!'

And how she lectured Mum! 'Now, Janet, you're far too soft… it's time these weans were taught a few lessons about responsibility… you can't run this house all by yourself…they're old enough to at least take charge of their own personal things and help you with day-to-day chores. Either that or you'll have to get paid help – maybe someone in the village could use the money.'

Mum, mouth twitching with desperation, responded, 'I've tried that, Peggy. Three different women have started but none of them could cope wi' this rag-taggle bunch.'

'Well, I'll cope,' Peggy announced, pursing her lips and glaring at no one in particular. Then she made a list of duties and orders as long as the hallway and stuck it on the kitchen door.

My mother's attitude to cleaning was 'Och, just give it a wee wipe…that'll be fine.'

Peggy's was 'Clean it till you can see your face in it.'

By the end of the first day, the Glory Hole was empty and bare. Piles of our treasures lay stacked and classified in the back garden, some ready for storage in a neighbouring hut and some to be taken to their final resting place at the local rubbish dump.

A retired painter from the village distempered and stippled over the walls with enough coats of soft pastel shades to obliterate the battleship-grey paint, and Mum busied herself making lacy curtains. The next thing was a removal truck arrived with beds, bedding and wooden tea chests full of our visitors' belongings.

The wooden chests were immediately assessed as new, unexpected resources. We saw fortresses…shops…a theatre and stage. We started planning variety shows using the tea chests for stage settings and props and, when they'd been emptied, we carted them to the farthest corner of our property.

Peggy worked from early morning to past our bedtime in every room in the house. She cleaned, washed and polished anything that got in her way of domestic perfection. Before the invasion, the surfaces of sideboards and little tables had been popular resting places for books, games, half-made models and half-mended clothes – and layers of dust. Suddenly they became shiny mahogany and cedar supports for reading lamps and china ornaments.

Peggy was a part-time ogre. She was also a great teacher. In line with her favourite mantra, 'A place for everything and everything in its place', she allotted each of us personal space for our belongings and, in spite of her domineering attitude, I began to like this new arrangement. I liked wearing clean, ironed clothes. I liked to see the wood grain in our beautiful furniture become visible with a bit of attention. I discovered that I liked things to be clean and tidy. I especially liked having my own space and knowing that my books had a spot for safekeeping.

I learned from Peggy that organisation saved a lot of time. I learned that there were more efficient ways to look after one's treasures and belongings. Mostly I learned that happiness comes in many forms and that structure and discipline have their own rewards.

When the war ended, Peggy and her dearies left Scotland and returned to their home in Canada. Seagoing trunks and new wooden tea chests were packed and picked up by the shipping company. The last room on the left at the end of the lobby was empty again. Although, by the time the *Castel Felice* had left the port of Greenock with our Canadian cousins, our Glory Hole was in the process of being restored to its old days of chaos. But now we had lovely coloured walls and lace curtains and the sticker on the door said The Palace.

'Mrs McKendrick? Mrs McKendrick, Doctor McLelland will see you now.' The voice penetrated my fantasy. I flapped my eyelids and focused on the white uniform and smiling face of the nurse. The magazine, still open at page forty-six, had slid to the edge of my lap. I took a last look at the picture, closed it and placed it on the table in front of me.

The nurse looked puzzled as I dabbed the corner of my eyes with a tissue.

'Are you okay?' she asked.

'Yes…yes, I'm fine, thank you. I think I dozed off,' I said, following her into the dentist's room.

Unchained

My shoes lay where I'd kicked them off my tired feet and I'd changed my nurse's uniform for comfortable tracky pants and a loose jumper. A run of six night shifts at the aged care centre had left me feeling like the tired old tart he said I was and I'd been looking forward to this respite since leaving work an hour earlier. Whiffs of fresh coffee percolating made saliva gather in my mouth and slide along my tongue.

I'd just sipped the first warm sweetness and stretched out on the lounge with the latest *Women's Weekly* when the clanging sound of the doorbell shot out of the stillness – like a canon fired during a silent funeral service. I jumped. Coffee spots splattered onto the glossy pages. Bugger! Bugger! Thinking it might be the agent of some obscure religion, I waited.

The bell rang again. Persistent. S'pose I better answer it…might be some divine being who'll lead me out of this hellish life.

I'd been reading an article about how to change the bits of your life you were unhappy with. 'You are the architect of your own life,' it stated. 'Ask yourself – what do you want to see happening here? And what can you do about it?' Yeah, sure! I hated the shape my life had taken since I'd moved in with him.

Only yesterday I'd asked him if he'd like to go away for a few days. 'I'll organise flights and accommodation. You don't need to do anything.' I'd pleaded.

'Nah…got plans o' me own,' he'd sneered from our rumpled bed, scratching his belly as I stood in the doorway ready to leave for work.

That's how it was with him…the man who called me 'Hey, you' when he wanted something to eat or money for the pub. After our first few months together, his lovemaking had become a swift sweaty beer-smelling tumble, a spasm, then the sound of his snorting and snoring in drunken sleep. Sometimes I'd slip out of bed and watch a movie or read. Other times, I'd lie awake trying to push the sounds and smells of him away from me while my body screamed for satisfaction and my heart grew empty and cold from neglect.

I'd been thinking about these things on the way home from work and defeat had settled around me squeezing the life out of me like octopus tentacles around my ribcage.

'You are the architect...' Am I?

I padded barefoot to the door and looked through the spy-hole. 'Who are you?' I asked the face.

'Rosco Deloit, I need to talk to Jack Dunbar.'

'What d'you wanna talk to him about?'

'I represent ABC Finance Company. I need –'

'Sorry, he's not home.'

'You Mrs Dunbar?' he asked.

'Close enough,' I spat.

'Would you mind opening the door?'

'Don't know. Why? What did say your name was?'

'Rosco. Rosco Deloit,' he told me again and held up to the spy-hole a plastic card showing his photo ID.

I slid the security chain along a track on the door jamb, at the same time kicking the shoes and junk mail scattered around the entrance into a pile.

Rosco Deloit was a short stocky man with black greasy hair and skinny dark eyes. He was dressed in a business suit, a white shirt and a tie that had been loosened away from his opened top shirt button. The stench of garlic punched my nose and I stepped back from the assault.

'What d'you want?' I asked again.

He tapped a dirty fingernail on a blue document. I looked down at two pudgy hairy hands.

'This is authorisation to re-possess a TV and sound system.'

My shoulders slumped. I reached out my hand. 'Show me.'

He handed me the sheaf of papers. 'This is a copy of the contract signed by your husband. He's defaulted on the repayments and unless you can make a payment of five hundred dollars within twenty-four hours, the goods'll be recovered and auctioned.'

I glanced at the legal jargon while doing a quick reality check on my finances. My credit card was over its limit and the last withdrawal on my everyday card had left a balance of twenty-seven dolars. Another four days before I'd be paid again.

Often it had seemed to me that my wages swirled like a vortex into alcoholic fumes and cigarette smoke. He had laughed at my worries about money before going off to the pub with his mates when he should have been looking for a job.

'What do you want to see happening here?' What did I want to see happening…?

I looked into the lounge. A shaft of light splayed from the window onto the wide-screen TV that faced his chair, still showing the impression of his fat frame. Then, from somewhere, as if the sun had turned a light inside my head, I felt myself coming alive. I pushed up the sleeves of my old jumper and tucked a wayward strand of hair behind my ear.

'Tell you what,' I said, 'phone whoever you need to and ask them to bring a van to pick up the stuff.'

When Rosco Deloit left, I made two phone calls. One to my friend Milly, and one to my brother Stan.

'That's the best news I've heard in years, Mel!' Milly screamed. 'I'll be there as fast as the traffic will let me. Is there anything you want me to pick up on the way over?'

'Yes…boxes…plenty of them.'

Twenty minutes later, she arrived with her sister, another friend and two cars filled with flattened cartons.

Stan said he'd be over when he finished work and that I could use his other flat as long as I needed to.

By three o'clock that afternoon, Milly and company had left and a van and truck were lined up in the driveway. I watched as the plasma screen, stereo, speakers and DVD player were loaded into the van. The young driver looked sheepish when he asked me to sign something before speeding off to the world of re-possessed goods.

I watched the white doors of the van shrink as it followed the road and imagined a building somewhere…something like an airplane hangar filled to the rafters with reclaimed goods. I was wondering what the sound would be like if all the stereos lying there were tuned into a classical music station on full volume, when Stan's voice pulled me back to the practicalities of the moment.

'Hey, dreamer…what do you want packed next?'

For the next hour, Stan, and a friend who'd come with him, loaded furniture, boxes of dishes, linen, appliances and clothes into Stan's truck. When they loaded the recliner chair, I thought about the delusions I'd had for a 'happy ever after' kind of life when I'd bought the chair. It'd been the day after we'd first slept together. Then I remembered the worst thing about him, his weakest point: he didn't have a conscience; something I didn't understand until after the chains of commitment shackled me to him.

I looked around the empty rooms and it was like watching the links in that chain separate as if they were made of paper. At the same time, the rope that connected me to better times, before he'd bulldozed his way into my life, was suddenly spliced into something more supportive and stronger than anything in this house.

Before closing the door for the last time, I went out to the truck and, pointing to a small rattan chair, I said to Stan, 'I'll take that back.'

'Okay…you know what you're doin'.' He put the chair on the footpath.

I humped it back to the lounge and put it in front of where the TV had been, scrawled a message on a piece of paper and stuck it on the wall with Blu-tack. The last thing I saw before closing the door was the TV program lying on the floor beside a blue document. The first thing he'd see when he came home was a notice written in bold black ink saying, ENJOY THE VIEW.

New start for Jack

I watch Dave's car speed off and fumble in the dark with my keys. Usually the porch light is switched on. Maybe she's foolin' around with my head again. She loves playing games…elite level. The plant pots are missing from the porch. Maybe she's sold them or gave them to… nah, she'd never give anything unless the payoff was worth it. Heavy metal music still thumps in my head and my throat feels like it's been sandpapered raw.

None of the usual junk clutters the hallway and at first I don't notice the phone sitting on the floor or that the little table we'd bought at a second-hand store is missing. I'm so tired and head straight for the bedroom, hoping she'll sleep through my getting into bed. I can't handle another row or another session of her complaints about money or finding a job. I stop sharp at the bedroom door, stand there gaping like a dressed up dummy in a men's shop window. No fuckin' bed! No fuckin' furniture! No fuckin' her! My stuff that was usually scattered on the dresser and things that I kept in the drawers are stacked on the floor of the open wardrobe. My head can't get around what my eyes are seeing.

I wander into the lounge to have a think and take a sledgehammer hit to my gut! My chair is gone. The TV – gone. Everything. My music collection…everything. I see a bit of paper stuck to the wall. 'Enjoy the view' it says. The stupid cane chair she'd bought in one of her fits of home decorating sits in front of it. I pick the chair up and heave it at the wall. The cushion falls at my feet. It looks like a dead dog. I grab it, hold it close. A faint fragrance batters my nose like a cannon shot. I slide to my knees and weep like a five-year-old kid on his first day at school. Even in her absence she can grind out my guts.

Lying on the floor, I try to fathom how and why it has all come unstuck. When did I stop being enchanted by her face…by her energy? When had the laughter stopped? I want to punch the walls so hard that they'll fall down around me.

I check my phone for messages then remember that we'd stopped texting each other months ago. S'funny, I'd kept her last message in my in box: 'Did you get the job?' I toss the phone to keep company with the chair and sink into the good times we'd had.

Dave, my DJ friend, often asked me to help him out at weddings and twenty-first birthdays. We worked well together, bouncing jokes off each other and revving up the atmosphere. This particular Saturday we'd been at a wedding venue since five o'clock and the tables were starting to fill up. A buzz of conversation was building above the soft, lead-in kind of music. One of the tables was encircled by a bunch of women chattering on about whatever women talk about – prob'ly hair, shoes, Oprah. I heard one of them call out, 'Mel, over here!' and in walked the prettiest face I'd ever seen. She was tiny – not more than five feet in the old measurement. A red ruched dress, with spaghetti straps showing just enough cleavage to keep me guessing, clung to her body. Shiny black hair, scrunched and frizzy, sat on her shoulders and wreathed her face.

I stared at her – it was like that ad for Cash Converters where the bloke's eyes bulge and his tongue spears out about fifty centimetres from his face. I'd always been a leg man, but decided then and there that even if her legs were mottled, bowed and fat, it wouldn't matter.

Dave shouted, 'Hey, Dunbar…can you help with this?'

For the next while I was distracted by CDs and the music menu but my eyes kept pulling themselves back to the face above the red dress, like they were running out of their holes and back again.

When guests ventured on to the dance floor, I asked Dave to play Chris deBurg's 'Lady in Red' and started the long, long trek across to where she sat. I couldn't believe my luck when she smiled. That face… her face! It sparkled like electric cars! My eyes watered.

We danced close…closer and closer still, until her head rested in the perfect spot on my chest. She laughed when I signalled Dave to play it again. He mouthed a big 'NO!' and she deserted me to join her friends. I couldn't tell Dave that I still felt her in my arms and smelled her hair – he'd think I'd gone all soft.

Later, she joined me on the stage to help Dave pack up. When we'd finished and the guests had gone, she agreed to an end of night drink in the lounge bar. We talked music. We talked about things we liked. She told me her full name was Melanie Ann Davidson. We talked and laughed until three in the morning.

Within a month we'd found a house to rent and spent the first weeks of our new life decorating and furnishing and loving each other morning noon and night. We argued a lot about music. She liked Michael Buble and when I heard 'Come Fly With Me' it reminded me of my mother's old Frank Sinatra tunes – it sounded like the dreary background stuff played for funeral home ads.

Our first big battle ended with an agreement that she'd listen to her stuff when I was out and I'd listen to Oscar Peterson or James Morrison when she was out.

For the first months of our life together, my day job was all about conferences, breakfast meetings and new car releases. She came along when her work schedule allowed but she never really seemed interested. She couldn't hold a conversation with any of my colleagues…said she didn't know anything about the car industry. I remember saying things like 'Yeah, babe, they're a bunch of capitalist arseholes.' Then I'd feel guilty saying those things about people who'd encouraged and promoted me in an industry that gave us a very nice lifestyle, but I wanted to make this thing with her work.

The big blow to our good times fell when I became a victim of downsizing…restructuring…whatever. The redundancy package kept us solvent for a while and we still managed flights to five-star resorts for short holidays.

That's when the war began in earnest. Her nagging…my defence…

her shouting…my coaxing…her turning away from me in bed. 'There are heaps of jobs…you don't have to be a big-wig,' she'd say like a puffed-up adder of superiority.

My search for work made me realise two things. Firstly, there were no jobs available at the level of pay she wanted; secondly, the car industry was in the doldrums and most of the people I knew were competing for the few jobs available. My pages of contacts became a mass of crossed out, blacked out names and numbers. Dave gave me some work; most times he hardly needed me.

She'd get the careers section of the paper and highlight in pink jobs she thought were suitable. She'd point and announce, 'The Public Service is secure,' and make another pink circle. She'd bludgeon me about money. 'I'm working my ass off so you can spend your time in the pub…I'm working to keep you…blah, blah blah.'

I stopped eating at home. She went on permanent night shift. I put my car under wraps in the garage.

Once, she suggested going away for a few days to a resort we'd stayed at when life was brilliant, but I couldn't handle her paying for flights, accommodation and making the arrangements. I told her to piss off on her own if she wanted, I'd other things to do.

That morning, the bang of the door slamming reminded me of the backfiring sound from my first old car. I knew she'd be stomping down the pathway and flinging her anger around at the car door and her sports gear and work stuff and I sneaked a look through a chink in the curtains. Her face contorted, lips screwed tight, eyes shining like they were made of flint and burning red coals. I felt dead from the feet up.

Now, in the emptiness, I can't remember the last time I felt alive.

Dave has just arrived home when I phone. Before I tell him the whole story, he says, 'I'm on my way. See you in ten. Lynn's coming too.'

I stand up when they arrive. My knees are wobbly and my head spins as if I'm coming out of a drunken stupor. Dave looks at me with his mouth open and his forehead crumpled like a dried-up potato.

Lynn hugs me so tight, I nearly stop breathing. 'I'm so sorry, Jack. I can't believe she'd do this. You were so generous. The holidays. The clothes. The jewellery. Did she leave you anything?'

'I'm tellin' ya,' I spit, 'if I knew where she'd gone…' I pace the floor.

'Mate, what can you do about it? How 'bout you come back to our place?' Dave says from a corner, arms hugging his knees.

'I won't mind,' Lynn says. 'You can bunk in our spare room until you sort things out.'

'Sort what fuckin' things out?'

'Well, maybe…'

'No way, Lynn. She's done. Finito. Scrapped.'

Dave who's been wandering through the rooms, calls out, 'Hey, Dunbar, have you checked the garage and shed?'

We troop outside. Switch on the light in the garage.

'Thank Christ…she's left my car. At least I've got that.'

Dave points to the rear window. 'Hey, Jack, look in here.'

The rear seat is full to the top with boxes of CDs and my old collection of albums lie on the front passenger seat, with more on the floor.

We check the garden shed. Besides all my tools, it's crammed full of my model car collection. It's worth thousands and the envy of my rev-head friends. At the start, she'd insisted on displaying it in a glass cabinet she bought especially. Then when things had started to go bad, she demanded I relegate it to the shed. I haven't looked at in months.

We spend the next hour loading stuff into Dave's car. I take another look inside, close the door, back out of the driveway and start a new life.

Lights out

Six friends lie on lounges or sit on rattan chairs. The dusk that encircles them obscures the lemon geranium bush and frangipani tree that scent the air. Jack sips the last of his cab sav. Vivian fusses with dishes of nuts, pita bread, pâté and chunks of yellow cheese cubed like miniature marble slabs.

Dave, legs straight out and ankles crossed with a glass of wine in one hand, fly swat in the other, slouches and watches. Now and again he stabs at the night saying, 'Gotcha! bloody pest!'

Earlier ,the group had been to Henley-on-Sea for a pasta meal to celebrate Kathy's thirtieth birthday.

Vivian asks, 'Anyone for coffee?'

'Yup, hot strong black,' Jack answers.

'Wouldn't mind tea. Ginger if you've got it, Viv,' Kathy says from behind a newspaper and sitting back from the group. Then to Dave, 'Would you please stop with the swatting, Dave, the breeze is disturbing my paper, and d'you like playing God with the lives of insects?'

'Yep, I do, it's like…'

Viv stops in front of Dave. Head back, chin out, arm sweeping across the gathering, she quotes, '"As flies to wanton boys, we are to the gods; they kill us for their sport."' With a sideways tilt of her head she swans Maggie Smith style towards the kitchen. The group applauds.

Then, from Lynn, 'Let's have a game of charades or something. Life's too short for sittin' around doin' nothing.'

Kathy looks over the top of the paper. 'Hey, listen to this! "What you eat today walks and talks tomorrow," this health guru says. What d'you think about that?'

'Bollocks!' Fat Barry shouts from the kitchen window. 'When

d'you ever see a pizza wi' legs? Hey, Viv…better watch that cheese…
might start talkin' to you!'

Lynn picks up a piece of pita bread. Holding it in front of her
mouth, she says, 'Hello, would you and your pals like a game of Trivial
Pursuit?'

Kathy grabs another bit of bread, folds it to make a mouth and
asks, 'Name the baker who started the Great Fire of London,' she
chortles, opening and closing the bread in time with her words.

'Don't know his name,' Lynn answers, 'but it started in Pudding
Lane because he hadn't doused the oven fires.'

Jack picks up an empty wine bottle, and says to the label, 'What
patch of Wirra Wirra did your grapes come from?'

Barry whispers from behind him, 'Don't know…doesn't matter…
great drop.'

Dave abandons the fly swat and joins in the fun. 'What Australian
state has the highest fatal accident rate?' All states and territories get a
mention before they give up.

Viv puts a tray of drinks on the coffee table in the centre of the
patio. She stands back laughing as questions and answers on TV
personalities, rock music, titles and authors of books get fired across
from one to the other. She pretends to keep score until they run out of
questions and collapse with teary laughter.

'Well, that sure got us going. Good fun,' Lynn says, taking a bite
of bread. 'I'm so glad we made the effort to get together. It's been too
long since the last time.'

'I've had a great time,' Kathy says. 'Thank you, but I gotta go.' She
reaches for a lime-green tote and brushes her fingers through her hair.

'Have a great birthday tomorrow, Kath. Enjoy your day,' they
chorus as she follows her shadow to the edge of patio lights calling out,
'Goodnight all.'

Jack and Lynn follow, saying, 'Early rise tomorrow.'

'I'll stay and help Viv clean up,' Barry pipes up.

Dave laughs, 'Generous of you, Bazza, seein' as you live here.'

They blow air at each other with promises to catch up again soon. Vivian starts cleaning up platters, red-stained glasses and bottles with sediment stuck to their sides. The patio lights are switched off to the sound of departing cars.

Barry puts both arms around Viv and snuggles his face into her neck. 'Leave them till morning, babe,' he coaxes, and starts pulling her gently towards their bedroom.

Before they take another step, there's a screech of tyres, a loud thud like an explosion, the sound of metal crashing and the hoot and whistle of a security system. Barry grabs his mobile phone and runs towards the noise. He sees Dave standing stock still on the kerbside staring at his feet. Then he sees a personal organiser, phone, notebook, keys, cosmetic bag. Stuff that's spewed from the mouth of a lime-green tote. He sees motionless fingers curled around a handle.

There is a moment when all that can be heard is the stertorous breathing of Barry and Vivian. A moment when the street light illuminates the shards of glass stabbing Kathy's face. A moment before blood starts sliding, gushing, spurting from her wounds. Then the sound of steam hissing from the engine of a car that's impaled on a stobie pole. Wailing. Sobbing. Sirens hurtle through the night towards them. Barry stoops to Kathy's body. Five friends huddle behind him as he frantically tries, but fails, to find a pulse.

Redemption

3 June 2006

Heathrow Airport

The fuzzy feeling in my ears from the descent partly blankets warnings about unattended luggage. People in transit stay so close to their bags they are almost glued together. Waiting for my flight to Glasgow I take in the sounds and sights around me. People of all nations walk and wait. I see Africans in bright togas and turbans, Indians in saris, Scots in kilts and a Texan or two.

In the corner, on a wooden bench, three women sit quiet beneath full, black chadors. Eyes, like jet beads darting here and there and occasional movements under the fabric, are the only signs of life. An old man with a pockmarked face stands in front of them holding a bunch of documents that looks like passports and boarding passes. A group with Deutsche Travelland name tags and bags discuss in loud guttural accents the inconvenience of their delayed flight. It is a wonder to me that some kind of order emerges from this bedlam and propels passengers to their destinations.

I am at the centre of the world. The idea that I am a short distance from the roads that Cromwell's army marched in the fight against royal absolutism astonishes me. I ponder the consequences of the Civil Wars and the impact that mass migrations in the search for religious freedom has had on this land.

'Flight CA25 London to Glasgow.'

A few steps through a connecting tunnel to the plane remind me of the children arriving in Narnia through a wardrobe.

Suddenly I am in Scotland! The soft accents of the flight attendants remind me of Mum and I wonder why she has never wanted to return to her homeland. Getting settled and grasping a tenuous connection to my Celtic origins is making the journey pleasant. Another reading of Aunt Lizzie's letter reassures me that this detour on my way to Spain will be rewarding.

Morar
West Highlands
Scotland
20 May 2006

My dear Christina

Thank you for the photo of your graduation. You look just like your mother did when I last saw her. Thank you also for making the time to spend with us. Ewan and I are eager to see you and to hear all your news about your mum and dad.

We have made reservations for two nights at the Erskine Bridge Hotel for you. We are known to the manager there and he will assure your comfort. It will give you a chance to recuperate from the long journey from Australia and some time to explore the city. Your interest in things classical will be stimulated with a visit to the Burrell Art Collection in Pollock Country House. It is a diverse collection of Greek bronzes, and some original works by Giovanni Bellini. For something surreal and modern, it may be worth a visit to the Kelvingrove Art Gallery, where Dali's *Crucified Christ* has a prominent position.

We are very proud of your achievements and impressed that you are presenting a thesis at a world forum. We have been to Spain many times and we will be happy to recommend good eating places and galleries that you might find interesting.

Ewan will pick you up at the hotel around 10.30 on the morning of 5 June. You can't fail to recognise him if I tell you that he looks like an eighth-century Viking. He is my gentle giant. Give my love to your mum and dad and have a safe journey.

Love from Lizzie and Ewan

4 June 2006

Kelvingrove Art Gallery

Dali's representation of Christ reminds me that there is a connecting chain from the beginning of Christianity through the English Civil Wars to the present day that keeps religious bigotry alive. The surrealist Christ figure is suspended in light as if he has risen above the evils of the world. Dali's Jesus seems to have rejected the shortcomings of humanity while the world's grim secrets are hidden from the light.

Late evening

Erskine Bridge Hotel

From my window I can see the beginning of the road I will take to my destination in the Western Highlands. It starts on the far side of an elegant bridge across the River Clyde that flows fast and deep beneath it.

I feel an excitement that I can't describe. It's like starting on a quest without a road map. Will Lizzie look like my mother? She is two years older than Mum and I know that they were great friends until Mum was sent away to live with her English grandmother. That time of her life is shrouded in vague answers to my questions about what she did there, how she spent her teenage years and how she and Dad met. Now, in the country of her birth, these questions have popped to the front of my mind again.

5 June 2006

En route to Morar

Ewan's bulk almost filled the hotel foyer. My hands, like those of a small child, disappeared when he took them in his.

He embraced me. Held me close, stepped back and looked at me. He studied every feature of my face like a man hungry for the sight of someone dear. 'Your eyes and hands are exactly like your mother's,' he said. He hugged me again and it was like I was disappearing into the heart of him.

He sits quietly beside me now concentrating on the narrow, convoluted roads. Place names on signposts are beguiling and I am remembering things I've read about clan wars and treachery fought through the centuries in the towns we pass. Just there is the road that leads to Culloden Field, site of the last battle fought on British soil.

The road is like a ribbon thrown carelessly around mountains that dominate the land and lift high above the tree line. It takes us through places with names written in Gaelic and English and the further north we go, Gaelic takes precedence on directions. Places like Crianlarich, Glencoe and Ballachulish are signposted.

Across Rannoch Moor, the valleys are covered in moss and lichen that looks like you would sink in it up to your knees. The moor spreads beneath craggy mountains with rivers that look like streamers of snow running from the summit. I am enchanted by the greenness of the valleys; silver shining on water; bold black mountains and the soft clean air of the Highlands. In the midst of all this grandeur and history there is an unexpected incongruence. A shop labelled 'Ben Wong – Purveyor of Turkish Kebabs and Fish and Chips.'

6 June 2006
Morar – midnight
We stopped at the Clanranald Hotel for lunch.

'Iain Ruadh,' the waiter said to Ewan as they favoured each other with a handshake.

Ewan discussed the menu with him in Gaelic and during the meal, I learned a few phrases of this lovely language.

I have never tasted salmon so sweet, so succulent. Lightly poached and served with a dill sauce, it was a superb example of Highland fare. When I told Ewan that the fish seemed to have jumped from the river onto my plate, he laughed.

'Well, Christina,' he answered, 'the breeding ground of the Spey is only a few miles from here and the Highlands are full of surprises.'

While we ate, Ewan asked if Mum was content with her life in

Australia. He asked if she ever talked about him and Lizzie. When I told him that they were very special people in our lives, his eyes shone like blue ice and a youthful face emerged from behind his whiskers.

Lizzie looks just like Mum. A little bit plumper and older but the same hair colour, height and complexion. She came running to the car crying big fat wet tears and threw her arms around me. Before Ewan had picked up my bags, she and I were sitting in the dining room sharing a pot of tea and the fattest scones I've ever seen. Amongst the photos she showed me I spied one of Mum and a young beardless Ewan. He is holding bicycle handlebars and Mum is sitting on the crossbar, both laughing into the camera.

10 June 2006
Morar

Today, we walked three miles to Mallaig to catch the boat for Skye. I was so engrossed in the vista of white houses nestling against green and black hills that I nearly missed what Ewan said.

He told me that Paul Longford was not my father. In his deep lilting Highland voice, he began the story of my mother's expulsion to Slough. 'Your mother was sixteen, your father eighteen. They loved each other dearly but your grandparents and the local priest would not bless the union because your father was not of the faith. Your mother deliberately got pregnant, hoping they'd be allowed to marry, but instead she was sent south to her grandparents.

'Your father, although he was not allowed to follow her or contact her, travelled secretly to England when he considered the time for your birth was near. He watched your grandparents' house from a rented room across the road every day for a week. At night he slept in a chair by an open window so that he would hear the sound of cars stopping in the street.

'It was close to midnight on Christmas Eve when the district nurse arrived. He walked across and stood at the side of the building out of sight, but within earshot of a lighted room that he guessed was where your mother lay. He stood outside until you were born early on Christmas morning. When he heard the sound of a newborn baby, he wept, gave thanks and returned to Morar the next day.

'Paul Longford had befriended your mother during the waiting time and when you were three months old they married and left for Australia.'

When I asked Ewan who this man was, he looked me in the eye and said, 'You will never hear that from me.'

Somehow I feel like a displaced person. My world has shifted. Everything around me has changed. I am standing at some strange juncture of my life thinking back to Dali's painting…the shades of dark and light…jaundiced religious views…the simple goodness shining through Ewan and Lizzie. Trying to process the details makes my brain whirl.

Lizzie evaded my questions about how she and Ewan met and where they were married. 'Och, I don't remember, lass…it seems he was always around and we just decided to be as happy as we could be in marriage.'

Like my parents, it seems that caring for each other has been the sole purpose of Lizzie's and Ewan's life.

14 June 2006

Departure from Morar

There are a hundred and twenty-three steps to a cross that sits on top of a hill overlooking Loch Morar. At this morning's first light, I sat there looking out to the west where, on a clear day, the distinctive shapes of the Hebridean islands Rhum and Eigg are visible. The pathway up to the cross is bordered by wild irises that glowed yellow in the early light and the fragrance of rhododendrons was all around me. The highland mist that falls almost daily, keeps the hill of the cross lush and green. White sands encircle the loch, and beyond that is the Atlantic Ocean. The hill dips down to the grounds of St Colum's church, where my mother and Lizzie were baptised and confirmed. And where, according to Lizzie, the priests still recite beatitudes and read sermons on brotherly love from their little books of prayer.

Tomorrow I will be in Pamplona. My heart is so heavy with the leaving of Morar, I won't be able to carry all of it away with me.

16 June 2006

Pamplona, Spain

My dissertation on the Co-existence of Differences in Seventeenth Century England was an academic success and I met some interesting people, but all this was secondary to the discovery about my birth. I feel humbled by the richness of my birthright. Today, I give thanks for the four wonderful people who dealt a blow to the wickedness of bigotry.

10 July 2006

Adelaide

Tonight as I watched my parents serve my welcome home dinner, I saw them smile and look clearly into each other's eyes. They asked homecoming questions like 'Was the airport crowded? Did you have a comfortable flight? What great new things did you discover?' I saw them move around the kitchen anticipating each other's actions and moving in unison. It was like watching two halves of one person dancing to the same tune. They almost look like each other. They will never know that I have guessed the price they paid for this happiness. I embrace both my families and am comforted by knowing that I belong in two beautiful corners of the world.

Lost saints

Hannah coaxed back the tears and croaked, 'Have a safe journey. Call me when you arrive back in Adelaide.' I slipped a small blue gift box into her coat pocket. We parted. At the top of the departure ramp I turned to look back. She waved. I waved and wondered when we'd meet again.

In the departure lounge, I rummaged for my notebook and, while waiting to board, I re-read the daily record of my visit.

During the two weeks we'd just shared, we'd gone through a box of photos of our teenage years. Some showed us in seersucker shirt-waisted dresses, posing with guitars and beehive hairdos. We laughed and cried about the big things and little things we'd experienced on our separate life journeys. The times when we'd pleaded sick and taken an afternoon off work to watch Elvis in *Love Me Tender* – and how we'd sobbed when his dying image faded from the screen and the words of the song poured over us.

Hannah and I had been friends since we sat side by side in primary school as five-year-olds. All through our school years we'd been neck and neck in exam results. She'd be first, I'd be second, or vice versa. We shared dux of the school before starting our secondary education.

At the start of my holiday, we cried over whisky nightcaps and shared stories. She talked a lot about the loss of her seven-year-old son and I told her about living alone since my man's death two years earlier.

One evening when we'd been to a social event at her local club, Hannah's unwavering belief that she was protected totally by the saints we'd grown up with in a Catholic childhood became a point of angry disagreement. 'I can't accept that Saint Anthony will find that lost sock. I can't agree that if I make a novena to Saint Cecilia, I will have success as a renowned pianist. And I most certainly can't believe that God will pay my rent!'

I picked up my drink and started pacing. 'Look at it this way, Hannah: who supported you when Peter died? Who looked after your other children when Alex died?'

She sipped her drink and looked at me as if I'd committed sacrilege of the highest level. 'Clare, what you've just said horrifies me. It's more than a venial sin.'

'Venial? Mortal? Sacrilege? I don't know about these things any more. All I know is that we are responsible for ourselves and the welfare of our children. God doesn't do the hard yacka that puts food on the table.'

'No, but he presents the opportunity for you to do it.'

The look she gave me was like the sudden flashing of a light through a pitch black night. The argument developed into a fracas. I felt it happening like symptoms of an illness coming on.

I heard myself say, as if it were some other woman, 'I'd never pray to a god who took my son from me. God's will is imposed on you so profoundly, Hannah, you can't even break out of the constraints because you don't even know they're there!'

In the end, we agreed to disagree and planned some touring trips that would fill in the time until my departure.

Hannah reached the exit doors at the same instant as a flying, flaming green Jeep. While my plane circled Dubai airport, forensic personnel were searching the debris for body parts. All that was found of Hannah, was a little blue box. Inside it, a tiny gold medal of St Christopher.

Written on 30 June 2007, the day of the terrorist attack on Glasgow airport.

The prodigals

Sunday afternoon and force-six winds are whistling through the branches of an ancient pine tree at the back of our yard. Old Dougie, my next-door neighbour, has invited me in for a cup of tea and a chat. I'm pushing the rusty wrought-iron gate in the back fence to a close when my mobile phone nearly jumps out of a side pocket in my jacket. At that very instant, Dougie appears on his back veranda chortling at the sight of me with the phone in one hand and the other trying to tame my skirt that's flapping around like some wild thing. The hood of my jacket has blown off and I imagine my hair looks like a flattened, wet bird's nest.

'It's Matt and Steve,' I call out. 'They're at the end of the expressway and want to stop in.'

'Tell them to come here,' Doug answers. 'Haven't seen them in ages.'

When my boys were little and their father still alive, Doug's three girls and my boys spent a lot of time together. On weekend evenings while the young people watched movies or played ball games outside, the adults played canasta or Scrabble, or sometimes we'd work on jigsaw puzzles. Esther, Doug's wife, was especially good at them. At those times, Esther and I would speculate on engagements and weddings that would make us into one big family with shared grandchildren. But Esther got cancer and died and my Pete succumbed from burns he'd collected during the bushfire season of 1983. This all happened before Doug's girls moved overseas and my boys set off in search of life partners.

'Me neither,' I shout above the noise of wind and rain. 'I'll be back in a jiffy.'

Earlier, I'd made a crock full of ham-bone soup with heaps of vegetables like I used to do in the years when I'd four hungry menfolk to feed. These days, though, I fill meal-size containers, take a few in to Doug and freeze some for myself for those times when I don't feel like cooking. Today, for some reason, I'd left the full pot on the draining board at the edge of the sink.

I collect a pack of bread rolls from the freezer, a family size chocolate bar from the pantry and a stack of serviettes. I stack them into a green bag and leave it beside the soup. The rain coming down in big fat wet plops bashes the patio roof and the pavers beyond the decking. I see water seeping under the warped door of my garden shed and make a mental note to remind my sons – for about the hundredth time – about fixing the door like they'd promised.

I phone Matt. 'Pick up the bag and the pot of soup before coming into Doug's,' I yell, above the din that's pouring from his car radio, and set off once again.

This time I take my umbrella – stupid move: it blows inside out and gets jammed between the fence post and the gate. I leave it lying there like a giant, dead, red, silk-covered spider.

I'm standing on Doug's porch struggling out of my sopping wet jacket and pushing hair away from my eyes when Matt's RV arrives in my driveway. A few minutes later the boys thump into the warmth of Doug's kitchen loaded with food. As well as the soup and green bag, they have a huge chocolate mud cake, four different cheeses, Kalamata olives and a jar of New Zealand mussels.

'What's all this stuff?' Doug asks, grinning, his eyes shining like he'd been given an award of some kind. 'I thought you were coming in for a cup of tea?'

'Went to the market yesterday,' Steve tells us.

Amidst a lot of shuffling and handshaking and a chorus of 'How you doin'?' and 'Fine, thanks,' I start setting crockery and cutlery on the dining room table.

I whisper from the side of my mouth to Doug, 'The prodigals have honoured us with a visit. We may as well make a feast of it.'

'Great idea,' Doug chortles, and shuffles off to the cupboard he calls his wine cellar.

A few minutes of clinking and he appears with a dusty bottle of red. 'Been savin' this for a winter day with company,' he says, holding the bottle aloft. 'I'm tryin' to mind the last time we sat around here bashin' each other's ears.'

Matt, setting wine glasses, says, 'Wasn't that long ago, Doug. Maybe Christmas?'

'Yeah…maybe…but that was six months ago.'

Steve pipes up, 'Nah, we saw you for Mum's birthday.'

I look at both of them. 'That was November, Steve.'

They look at me with the look they used to get when they were young and had been discovered in some boyhood prank.

'Never mind,' I say. 'You're here now, so let's make the most of it.'

For the next while, we eat and drink and talk about ordinary things like cricket and movies. It feels so good to hear their voices and I think I must look like Lewis Carroll's Cheshire Cat.

Doug says, 'I heard a funny thing the other day. A young fella, about seventeen, sitting on a windowsill outside the local Subway restaurant, says to his friend, a girl, "Hey, wanna hear about the wicked deal I got on my SIM card t'day?" "Sure," she answered, picking at the split ends of her dyed blonde hair. I didn't hear the rest but I thought to myself, what in the name o' the wee man is he talking about? What's a SIM card? What'd he mean, wicked deal?'

Matt piped up. 'It looks like your education in today's technology is sadly neglected, Doug. He was talking about his mobile phone. You should get yourself one.'

'What would an old codger like me do with a mobile phone? That one there works perfectly fine,' says Doug, jerking his thumb towards a handset on the wall by the kitchen door.

'Matt's right, Doug,' I tell him. 'They're real handy. You could have it in your pocket. Then if you have a fall, you can dial for help from wherever you happen to be. And it keeps you up to date with what's happening in the world.'

'But Sal, man has lived for thousands of years without a bloody mobile phone. Besides, they cost too much.'

'Not if you use it as often as you don't use that one,' I retort, sweeping my hand across in the direction of his phone.

My hand flicks Steve's half-full glass of red. Everybody jumps. Steve grabs the salt cellar, and starts shaking it over the spreading stain.

Matt gathers serviettes from here and there on the table and starts soaking up the wine. 'Should I squeeze this into a glass, d'you think?' he says, laughing at my panic.

'Don't worry, Sal,' Doug says. 'It'll come out in the wash.'

Between us, we clear the last of the dishes from the table. Doug slides the tablecloth off and Matt picks at the edges of the brown padded protector blanket beneath it.

'No, just leave that, will ya,' he cautions Matt. 'There's a surprise under this cover.'

Dougie shuffles his chair away from the table edge and slowly, slowly peels the cover off – the way you'd peel tissue away from a newly bought piece of Stewart crystal. The tabletop gleams.

'Twenty coats of lacquer on that,' Doug says, and strokes his hand gently across the biggest jigsaw puzzle I've ever seen.

It is a map of the world. Round. It defines countries, rivers and mountain ranges by colour.

'Wow! When did you do this one, Doug?' I ask.

'Well now, you think I'm falling asleep in front of the TV every night, dontcha?'

'Well, that's what most people your age do.' That's Steve joking.

Doug starts rummaging through a sideboard cupboard, at the same time tells us how the jigsaw came about. 'Alice sent me an atlas for Christmas a couple of years ago,' he mumbles, his head inside the cupboard. 'Here it is,' he says, lugging the tome from its hiding place and putting it on the table.

Alice, his eldest daughter, had put little yellow stickers on some pages of the book to mark the countries and cities she'd been to. Attached to these pages she'd paper-clipped typewritten notes explaining what she'd done there and a photograph or two of places she'd seen.

'When Alice sent me the atlas, I thought about how narrow my life has been. I'm too old to travel now and I wanted to make these sights more alive. So I took a map of the world to that wee printing shop on the corner. The young fella there copied it; enlarged it and made it into a jigsaw, the exact dimensions of this table top. Mind you, he had to do it in sections. What d'you think o' that?'

He points to a picture of Alice in front of a castle. 'See that? Blarney Castle. See how green the grass is,' he says, 'and here's another Irish site. See that stone she's sittin' on? That's, in the words of a song my father used to sing, the Stone Outside Dan Murphy's Door. And here's one of Kathy on Arthabasca glacier – that's in the Canadian Rockies.'

Steve points to an oversized vehicle parked behind Kathy showing her to be half the height of the wheels. 'Would you look at the size of that monster! Wonder how much replacement tyres cost.'

While they are ooohing and aaahing, I take another look at the tabletop. In a corner there are three different coloured ribbons. Blue with Alice written in black ink. Yellow is Deirdre and green for Kathy. At the spots on the map where each of the girls have been, there are tiny coloured dots.

'See, I don't need a phone to keep me in touch with the world. I have it all here at my fingertips.'

He shows us Deirdre in a London pub called the Pope's Grotto, Kathy sitting on the Spanish Steps in Rome at six o'clock on a summer morning, and both of them wearing jackets patched with a blue and white saltire, standing on the ramparts of Edinburgh Castle.

Before we know it, the sky is darkening. Doug moves to his leather recliner while Matt and Steve help me load the dishwasher.

The atlas lies open on top of the table. I take a last look before covering the world in padding and a clean white cloth. Over the map of Australia, Doug has pasted a photo of Esther and himself sitting on a bench in a garden. I hear a soft snore and glance across the room. I leave him to his dreams.

'Thanks for lunch, Ma. It was great to sit still for a while,' Matt says, giving me a big fat hug.

The three of us troop back through the rusty gate. The wind has dropped to a light breeze and an occasional drip, like a comma in a sentence, falling from roof gutters, is the only sign of rain.

'Yeah, Mum,' Steve smiles at me. 'Great way to spend a Sunday afternoon.'

'Glad you came. It's not often we get to sit around a table these days. And thanks for the contributions to lunch. When am I likely to see you again?'

They boys saunter out to the car. They turn around, shrug and call back to me, 'Soon, Ma, soon.'

Share house

As I tried to open the door to Augie's house, I realised that my mother's death had taken my sense of home and hearth away from me. I felt angry with her. All I wanted at that moment was to wrap myself in her presence. See the untarnished brightness in her face and hear her sing the morning into being, the way it used to be. I tried to recall when I'd last heard her sing and I wondered why I remembered the words of the songs but not the sound of her voice.

Getting soaked in the rain, trying to fit a bent key into an ancient lock to open a stubborn door, gave me a focus for my rage. I kicked and punched my way through feelings of longing for something that was irretrievable. Finally, the door gave up and I was in the hallway with water running off my jacket and soaking jeans sticking to my calves. I shuffled off my backpack, tossed it on the floor and hung my coat on a hook. A puddle formed beneath it and, as I moved into the kitchen, the tips of my shoelaces trailed a line of water worms along the wooden floor.

This old house had high metal-pressed ceilings, fancy lampshades, and tarnished brass fittings on the doors and windows. The kitchen, the first room on the left from the front door, was a long room with cupboards and shelves lining two walls. A bay window with small panes and a padded window seat, jutted out to a paved courtyard and a rose garden.

French windows on the north side opened onto a veranda where outside furniture, covered in plastic, was stacked into a corner. A long wooden table with ancient gouges and scratches over the surface dominated the room from the centre. It looked forlorn, as if waiting for company to sit around it in fellowship.

When I saw a skewed A4 sheet of paper with 'Welcome Karen' scrawled on it, slouching against a half-filled coffee mug in the centre of the table like an afterthought, I smiled. A biscuit tin on top of the fridge with Gainsborough's *Blue Boy* pictured on the lid, and labelled 'Kitty' held a bank of common funds for staples like coffee, tea and sugar. Sometimes the funds covered the cost of a shared pizza or Chinese takeaway when the housemates wanted a break from cooking.

Today is the first opportunity I'd had to see the house empty…a place where I'll live. Augie had told me that no one would be home at this hour but I hadn't expected the house to be so silent. It was cavernous. The sound of my footsteps on the wooden floors seemed to bounce off the walls and come back to me as if someone was walking beside me.

An ancient Olivetti typewriter sitting on a small two-tiered table with wheels at each corner was the communication centre of the house. The table looked like it could have begun its life as a trolley for serving sedate afternoon teas in a house named something like Rose Cottage.

I looked at the pile of past messages on the lower tier and realised that I had no history in this house. The rooms in Augie's house had nothing of me in them – the walls held none of my past. I wanted to shout a name or sing out an anthem to drown out the silence that overpowered me. I noticed my name had been pasted on a cupboard door between those of Joe and Mardi and felt a vague sense of belonging. Dented, stained containers on shelves beside the sink reminded me that Mel, Jesse, Steph and other past tenants had lived here. A bowl of pet food sat near the door waiting for Barney, the house cat.

While waiting for the kettle to boil, I watched the movement in the arms of a gum tree waving in the wind and listened to the sound of its branches scratching and tapping the window panes as if they too sought sanctuary. I opened and closed some cupboard doors and checked the fridge for milk. A half-full, still-warm pot of coffee sat on the base of the coffee maker

My friend Mardi had lived here for the past two years and had sometimes invited me to Augie's place to share a meal with the housemates and other friends. At those times we'd talk about our jobs or movies that were worth seeing. We'd eat the night away with wine and wit. Depending on how much wine was consumed, these confabs could last all night.

Rain pelting the windows. Hot, sweet coffee in a dry, quiet space. Lovely.

Mardi had coaxed me into moving to Augie's place. 'Being among new people will motivate you and get you back on track with your studies,' she'd said.

I sipped my coffee and turned my attention to the trees and plants I could see in the backyard. I tried to count the shades of green as they changed from wet silvery tones to greens of a translucent new-leaf tint, then almost black.

My mother had loved the colour green. She and I used to play at naming the many shades of green we found in our garden. Through the window, I could see what she'd called apple green, and a tone that looked like the underside of sage leaves. Emerald green shining on the wet leaves of a ginger plant reminded me of a slinky, silk shawl Dad had bought her in the Irish shop in the city. When she unwrapped the package, he'd draped it across her shoulders and Mum sang an Irish song about forty shades of green while they danced close together, the way teenagers did in the sixties.

I compared the tints on the foliage to the faded cornices in Augie's house that linked the ceiling above me to the kitchen walls. They looked more like the snot green of Joyce's sea in *Ulysses*. Thinking of that reminded me that a backlog of reading and writing waited in a box in the back of a truck that should've been here by now.

*

Ten minutes later, a blond boy jumped from the truck and started throwing my stuff onto the soggy leaves decomposing along the edge of the driveway. I pointed to a bag that I knew had dry clothes and shoes and asked him to get it for me.

'Sure – here 'tis,' he said, throwing it into my ribcage and nearly knocking me over.

After they'd gone, I swapped my wet things for dry socks and my old tracksuit. The splotches on my face made my skin look like that of an adolescent fighting hormonal adjustment – too many chicken and chip meals and chocolate bars. The quick change didn't do my appearance any good but I was dry and comforted. I thought I could smell the scent of home. I looked at the mess the movers had left, hoping that somehow the clutter would arrange itself. That the empty wardrobe would fill up by magic and my possessions would acquire the energy and motivation needed to transform into some kind of order.

I heaved and shuffled bags and cartons to make room against the longest wall for my computer desk, leaving space beside it for the bookcase. It felt good to be active and motivated. I managed to hook up the computer and switch it on and soon the sound of Robbie Williams singing 'Something Beautiful' blasted across the room from my CD player.

Arranging folders and binders labelled Renaissance Literature and Literature of the English Civil Wars on the bookshelves took a few minutes. I put Milton's *Paradise Lost*, two thick anthologies of English literature and paperback copies of poems by Donne and Herbert beside the notes. The titles reminded me again that I'd better get serious about my work.

'You can't manufacture a miracle…something beautiful will come your way…' the voice consoled me.

I stood admiring the results of my labour. I nearly jumped out of my skin when a voice roared above the music, 'I'm back!' I ejected the CD. The front door closed with a bang. Squeaks, groans and bumps from ratchets and ropes announced Augie's attempts at hanging his bike from butcher's hooks attached to a pulley in the hall. The clatter of dishes and the sound of the kettle being filled in the kitchen signalled time for a cuppa.

I'd liked Augie from the moment we'd met. I liked his open smile. I liked the way he looked into people's faces when he talked to them. I'd watch the smiles that followed him as if he had some subtle and secret ingredient that magnetised others around him. Dark-haired, sallow-skinned and slim-built, he was probably close to forty. He'd never been married but I had the feeling that tragedy lurked somewhere in his past – don't know why I thought that, there was nothing sad or dark about Augie. He made a living by teaching yoga in a studio attached to the back of the house. Three evenings a week and on Saturday mornings, the sound of bells and the hum of 'Ommmmmm' filtered through the walls minutes before a shuffling search for shoes signalled the end of sessions. He was also involved with street theatre and spent a lot of time mixing and moulding papier mâché into masks that he sold to arty groups around the city.

I joined him in the kitchen and while Augie opened cupboards to show me where crockery and kitchen things were kept, we talked about arrangements for housekeeping and meals. I lifted two mugs from a shelf, and made a pot of coffee.

He looked straight at me. 'You've been crying…you look a mess. Wanna talk about it?' He slid the sugar bowl and milk jug towards me and sat down at the other side of the table.

'Not now. Maybe another time.'

'D'you need help moving furniture?'

'Prob'ly. The removal men just dumped everything in my room and left – it's a shambles.' I took the biscuit he offered.

He leaned back in his chair, linked his fingers together and put his hands around the back of his head. 'Why'd you move here, Karen?' he asked.

'Don't know for sure. After Mum died, the house was too big…too empty. I tried music, two TVs, radio in every room at different volume levels – didn't matter how much noise I made, the house still felt like a morgue.'

Augie moved away from the table to check the cat's dish and rummage through the fridge for something to eat. 'Wanna sandwich?' he asked through a mouthful of celery.

'Mm, yes…great.'

I searched for a chopping board while Augie cut the rind from slices of ham and tossed it into the cat's dish. Together we built the best ham salad sandwiches on dark rye I'd tasted in weeks. While we ate, I told him about my success with the computer.

'Y'see, that's a small victory. What's the next step?'

'Finding places for things, I s'pose.' I ticked off a list of things to do on my fingers. 'I need to make space and arrange my uni work – make it accessible…set up my bed…put clothes away…separate things that could be stored…that'll probably take weeks.'

'How's uni?' he asked.

'Haven't touched my work in weeks.'

The front door opened and slammed shut.

Mardi waltzed into the kitchen loaded with shopping bags. 'Hi, Karen! I'm so glad you made it. I've been worried about how you'd manage. Did your furniture get wet? Have you had something to eat? Hi, Augie. Have you heard from Joe?' She rattled out the questions as if she'd popped the lid on the day's stored thoughts. She dumped her shopping on the floor and peeled off her coat then unwound a bright red scarf that looked to be about three metres long from around her neck and plonked down on the chair nearest me.

'Karen, take a look at what I've bought today.' She pulled out a black silk shirt and a flimsy shocking-pink camisole top. She held them against her chest then scrunched both of them in her hands. 'See – springs back – no creases – great for travelling, if I ever get around to it.'

'Hey, Mardi – fancy having a barbecue Sunday?' Augie asked.

'Sounds great. Who's cooking?'

'I am. But it'll be after we've helped Karen get herself organised.'

'I'll be there.'

'Sure you'll have the time?'

'Sure, I'm sure.'

We settled on seven o'clock Sunday and Augie said he'd invite a few friends around to meet me.

We were working out how much food we'd need when the front door slammed again and a voice bellowed, 'Fuckin' rain!' and feet clomped along the hallway.

'Joe's home,' Mardi and Augie said together and laughed.

I'd heard a lot about Joe but hadn't met him.

'Hi! Sorry about the language. You Karen?' He strode across the room to take my hand.

He threw his coat on the back of a chair, sat down and spread his arms, head and shoulders on the table. A tangle of frizzy ringlets around his face looked like they'd been sewn onto a woolly hat that met his eyebrows and smelt of wet dog. Raindrops dripped from a stringy beard that tried hard to cover his chin. He seemed to take up half the table. Drrrum…drrrum…drrrum – slap slap, went his fingers on the table like he was beating a bongo drum.

'Had a bad week? When'd ye get back? Would you like some coffee?' Mardi asked.

'Hang on, Mardi. One question at a time… Yes please, coffee. Hot and strong. I've been working with a bunch of fuckin' morons for the past three weeks.' He moaned, clutching his head.

'Hey, Joe,' Augie said, picking up a bit of paper from the pile under the Olivetti. 'Listen to this. Maybe you should stick it on the windscreen when you're driving to the next site.' He quoted, 'See the happy moron. He doesn't give a damn. I wish I were a moron… My God! Perhaps I am!'

We screeched with laughter. Joe threw his beanie across the table at Augie. It missed and landed on the cat's dish. I imagined the smell of ham settling amongst the threads of his hat attracting stray animals that would follow him, like the rats that followed the Pied Piper.

'They're not a bad bunch really,' he said when the hilarity died down. 'Three weeks is just too long in the field and I need a decent night's sleep.'

As if the sun had heard our laughter, and Joe's speech of contrition, it bounced through the windows and spread over the room, linking us together – like family.

Rolling the stone – an Easter story

There is a scar on my right knee – a white line about two centimetres long, now hardly visible amongst the wrinkles and other senescent marks. The blemish is a relic from a particular Easter Sunday that happened long before chocolate eggs and fluffy bunnies dominated supermarket aisles.

I lived in another country then, in a village where the week leading up to Easter was all about cleaning. Floors were scrubbed. Windows and their brass fittings buffed until they looked like slashes of sunshine. Wooden furniture was polished and the scent of Johnson's Lavender Wax seeped through every room. Carpets and rugs slung over the washing line in the yard and attacked with an ancient cane beater. When the front doorstep was freshened up with white paint, the clean up campaign was complete.

The fun part started on the night before Easter Sunday when my siblings gathered around the kitchen table to decorate hard-boiled eggs. Sometimes we'd boil the eggs in leftover tea to give them a tannish tinge. Then we'd arm ourselves with crayons, paints, scraps of coloured paper, tinsel if we could find any, and a tub of paste made with flour and water. We'd spend the evening wagging our chins at each other while drawing faces and flowers. Some of us made little paper skirts and tiny tinsel hats to be stuck onto the eggs. Before going off to bed at night, we'd line our masterpieces along the mantel shelf in the living room to wait for Sunday morning.

It was a time when women and girls wore hats and gloves for outings to the city or to visit relatives, a time when you wouldn't be seen outdoors on Easter Sunday without at least new shoes or a new hat. On Easter Sunday morning, the laneway leading to our church took the shape of a catwalk in a fashion parade. People preened and primped and nodded envy or admiration for their neighbour's taste in clothes.

One particular Easter, Mum or Dad must have had a win on the horses because everything I wore that day was brand new. A pretty straw hat with satin ribbon ties and daisies around the brim. A pale blue, princess-style coat over my first ever store-bought dress of candy striped gingham. My patent shoes, cotton socks and gloves were shiny white. I felt like I belonged to royalty.

On Easter Sunday morning, we usually went to early Mass before rushing home for breakfast. Then we'd make up paper bags of sandwiches and bottles of water and wrap our decorated eggs carefully in clean hankies and set off for the main event of the day.

Hill Sixty sat like a clump of overgrown vegetation at the edge of our village. It wasn't really a hill, more like a bump on the road with a few stumpy trees and straggly bushes. Anyway, it was the place where we usually played Cowboys and Indians, Tag and Red Rover. It had been named after some wartime skirmish. It seemed to me then that the walk to this spot took hours but on a recent visit back to my old haunts, I realised that the distance could be covered in less than ten minutes – no stretch of the legs.

After much jostling for position at the top of the hill and checking the downward slope for stones or holes that would stop the impetus, we'd place our eggs carefully in a row. Someone would yell, 'Go!' and we'd start rolling our eggs downhill. We'd shove and push and totter downhill while tap-tapping eggs on their way – all the while keeping watchful eyes on the competition. Grass stains and grazed knees were expected and ignored. Some of the smaller children would abandon the chase about the halfway mark. They'd plump down and eat their eggs. The only rule was, you were not allowed to lift your egg off the ground until it reached the end of the track. First to the bottom of the hill was the winner. The only prize was a glorious sense of victory while waiting for the others to reach the end of the slope. We were told that the meaning behind this ancient egg-rolling ritual was to symbolise the rolling of the stone away from the tomb of Christ after the crucifixion.

On my 'store-bought dress' Easter day, I was about halfway down the hill when a bully from my class shoved me too hard. I fell on top of my egg and my right knee landed on a sharp stone. I sat staring at the cut and screamed like a banshee when blood started oozing along my leg towards my new white socks and shoes. The bully ran off with my brother chasing after him.

Someone helped me to my feet and tied a hanky around the wound. Mum took me to the local doctor, who stitched the gash together. The yolk from the egg had turned a patch of my coat green and I cried more about that than the pain of getting my knee stitched. The bully's mother brought him to our door, holding him by the ear, and he was made to apologise. He gave me a Mars bar.

Over the years when I notice that scar, I remember the fun we had on Easter Sunday mornings. I remember too, the bully's stuttered apology. He's still apologising – swears it wasn't a shove but an endearing love pat. Next year we celebrate our fortieth wedding anniversary.

We totally agree on one thing: commerce has taken the fun out of Easter.